MY STORY
D-DAY

BRYAN PERRETT

D0993419

SCHOLASTIC

To Nathan and Niall.

While the events described and some of the characters in this book may be based on actual historical events and real people, Andy Pope is a fictional character, created by the author, and his story is a work of fiction.

Scholastic Children's Books,
Euston House, 24 Eversholt Street,
London NW1 1DB, UK

A division of Scholastic Ltd
London ~ New York ~ Toronto ~ Sydney ~ Auckland
Mexico City ~ New Delhi ~ Hong Kong

First published in the UK by Scholastic Ltd, 2004
This edition published by Scholastic Ltd, 2016

Text © Bryan Perrett, 2004
Cover photography © CollaborationJS, 2016

ISBN 978 1407 16543 1

Typeset by M Rules
Printed and bound in the UK by CPI Group (UK) Ltd, Croydon, CR0 4YY

2 4 6 8 10 9 7 5 3 1

The right of Bryan Perrett and CollaborationJS to be identified as the author and cover photographer of this work respectively has been asserted by them in accordance with the Copyright, Designs and Patents Act, 1988.

Papers used by Scholastic Children's Books are made from woods grown in sustainable forests.

December 1945

My name is Andrew Pope. Eighteen months ago, while commanding an infantry platoon, I took part in the Normandy Landings on 6 June 1944, a date that has now become known as D-Day. This is my story of how we prepared for D-Day, which was the greatest amphibious military operation in the history of the world, and of the fierce battles that took place once we were ashore, ending in the complete destruction of a German army. . .

1942–1943

I do not come from a military family although my great-grandfather, whose photograph we have, served as drummer boy during the Crimean War. He later served in India and other places around the world and retired as a sergeant major. During what is now known as the Great War my father served as an infantry officer. He was badly wounded on the Somme and again at Passchendaele, and he still has a slight limp as a result of his injuries. He rarely speaks of that war, which he regards as a horrible diversion from normal life. As he had seen almost all his friends killed or wounded, I can understand how he feels. When he left the Army he joined a firm of solicitors in Branchester, which is our county town.

I left school in 1942, shortly before my eighteenth birthday, having obtained good grades in my examinations. I was pleased that I had done particularly well in French and German, as these were my favourite subjects. It was then that I decided to volunteer for the Army rather than wait to be called up, because it seemed wrong to me that I should sit around doing nothing while the current war was going on, and anyway all of my school friends were doing the same. The war news was depressing. In North Africa, the British Eighth Army had sustained a serious defeat, Tobruk had fallen and the German Afrika Korps' runaway progress had been stopped with difficulty at a place called El Alamein, only 60 miles from Alexandria. On the Eastern Front, the German armoured divisions were carving their way deep into the Soviet Union and nothing the Russians did seemed able to stop them. At home, people talked about the opening of what they called the Second Front, which meant our army returning to France. Everyone knew that Hitler would only be beaten once this happened, and they looked forward to it because it would pay back the defeat we had suffered during the German invasion of France in 1940, followed by the Dunkirk evacuation. However, on 17 August 1942, a British and Canadian raid on the port of Dieppe was repulsed with heavy losses and it became clear that there would be no Second Front for a long time to come.

At the recruiting office that afternoon in 1942 I was told I would be sent joining instructions within a few days. My parents, of course, expected me to be called up sooner or later and I wondered how they would react when I told them I was going early. In the event, I didn't have much choice in the matter.

"Well, what have you been doing today?" asked my father after we had finished dinner.

"I've joined up," I said. "I was told that volunteers get a choice where they can serve, so I've asked to be sent to your old battalion, the 4th Branchesters, when I've finished my training. The sergeant said that there shouldn't be any difficulty because of the family connection. I was told that the battalion is on anti-invasion duties in East Anglia – having a rather dull time of it, apparently."

Father continued filling and lighting his pipe, regarding me in a way he had not done before.

"You've done the right thing," he said at length. "Just the same, I wish that you'd volunteered for something other than the infantry."

I knew what he was thinking. There had been times during the Battle of the Somme when the average life expectancy of a junior infantry officer in the trenches was two weeks.

"Things are different now, Dad," I said, little knowing what lay ahead. "We don't fight like that any more."

"Maybe," he replied, reflectively. "Nobody has used gas this time, thank God, but weapons are much more efficient than they were in my day."

He paused for a minute and I could see that he was thinking of the past.

"You'll meet some fine men, you know, fine men," he

4

continued. "You'll go for a commission, I suppose? You've had a good education and gained some experience in the school cadet corps, so in a way it would be shirking if you didn't put yourself forward as a potential officer."

"Yes, Dad."

"Good."

He puffed quietly on his pipe for a while, then looked me straight in the eye.

"You're right, of course, many things have changed a lot – but two haven't. First, remember that an officer's responsibility is to perform the task he has been set. Second, he'll never be able to perform it unless he has the trust and respect of his men. The only way he can earn that is by looking after them, seeing that they get fair treatment and being careful with their lives. Having said that, loyalty is a two-way street, you know. If three of my chaps hadn't taken terrible risks to bring me in from no man's land when I was wounded at Passchendaele, I wouldn't be here today."

There was nothing I could say to this, because he had seen a terrible war at first hand, whereas I had not. Seeing my serious expression, he gave one of his rare smiles.

"Don't worry, Andy, you'll be all right. Just don't go chasing medals or you'll give your mother a fit!"

Three weeks later I reported to a basic training unit. I found myself sharing a barrack room with men from many parts of the country and all walks of life. There were factory workers, farm labourers, clerks, tram drivers, accountants, builders and many more. Being away from home didn't bother me too much as, in a way, it was like starting a new term at school. I did, however, feel a little out of place among my companions at first. My own experience was confined to school and home, whereas they knew a great deal about life in the outside world. I asked them about their jobs and most of them seemed quite pleased that I was interested, telling me about their families, wives and girlfriends as well. They knew that I was classified as a PO (Potential Officer) and sometimes made fun of me. Some said they wouldn't want the responsibility of being an officer. Others that I was a fool looking for an early grave, but they were good-humoured and helped me out when I couldn't clean my kit when I was on fatigues (that is, in a working party, in the cookhouse or elsewhere). In return, I was able to help some of those who couldn't read or write properly with letters to and from their families. Because of my experience in the cadets I had no difficulty with such things as drill, weapons training and map reading. Physical training, constant exercise on the drill square, runs, route marches and the assault course made me fitter than I had ever been in my life.

In due course the squad completed its basic training and its members were posted to their various regiments.

I was sorry to see them go. While I was waiting to go before a WOSB (War Office Selection Board) I was given a short driving course. I was worried by the thought of the WOSB because it was a big hurdle and had the reputation of rejecting half of those who appeared before it. When I did attend I was subjected to three days of mental and physical tests during which my responses were carefully noted by officers on their clipboards. I did not think I had done at all well, but at the end of it I was summoned before the President of the Board and, to my relief, told I had passed. I felt as though I had won a major prize and telephoned my parents with the good news.

While all this was going on, the War had taken a turn for the better. General Montgomery's Eighth Army had defeated Rommel's Afrika Korps at El Alamein and was pursuing it across North Africa. It was beginning to look as though we might win the War after all.

In December 1942 I reported to the Officer Cadet Training Unit (OCTU) from which I hoped to pass out with a commission. On the first morning my company of new arrivals paraded wearing the white cadet bands around our forage caps. We all felt rather pleased with ourselves but were, in fact, about to enter the most ruthless phase of the selection process. For the next sixteen weeks we had barely a moment to ourselves. Our drill and uniform turnout had to be perfect at all times. As most of us were bound for the infantry, we had to learn the organization of an infantry battalion by heart. The battalion was commanded by a lieutenant colonel and consisted of six companies, each commanded by a major. Headquarters Company was responsible for administration and transport, while Support Company contained the battalion's mortars and anti-tank guns. The remaining four companies, lettered A to D, were rifle companies, each consisting of three platoons. Each rifle platoon was commanded by a lieutenant or second lieutenant, with a sergeant as his second-in-command, and contained three rifle sections.

Our cadet training began with our taking it in turns to command a section in attack and defence, and then a platoon. When we progressed to company tactics I began to realize that as future platoon commanders we were also being trained above that level so that if our company commander became a casualty we could at least take over for a while. We learned to dig slit trenches and the art of camouflaging ourselves and our positions. We learned about the different sorts of patrols we would have to lead and practised carrying these out after dark. Then there was advanced map and compass work, learning the basics of co-operation with tanks, artillery and engineers. There were lectures on army administration, our soldiers' pay and welfare, the enemy's weapons and tactics, current affairs, and how to give lectures ourselves when the time came. We were introduced to the relevant sections of King's Regulations, which govern how the Army is run, and the Manual of Military Law. There were many other subjects and throughout the course we were tested regularly to see how much we had absorbed.

The instructors, the company sergeant major and his sergeants harried us constantly, recording our progress in minute detail and discussing it among themselves. During one exercise, held in January, we were soaked by incessant rain by day and frozen when we tried to sleep in our slit trenches at night. I was sharing a trench with a former stockbroker named Guy Unsworth, who complained constantly. When we were told that the exercise would continue for another week, he gave full vent to his feelings.

"You got something to say, Mr Unsworth, sir?" snapped one of the sergeant instructors.

"Well, I mean to say, this just isn't on, is it Sergeant?" replied Unsworth in an aggrieved tone. "We're frozen stiff, soaked to the skin, and when the rations get to us they're stone cold. As if that isn't enough, when we try to eat them, our mess tins fill with rain. This whole thing has been badly organized in my opinion."

"That a fact, sir?" said the sergeant, eyeing him shrewdly. "I'll make a note of what you say."

In fact, when the exercise ended the following day, I

realized that the instructors had simply been testing our reaction to bad news. Shortly after, Unsworth and a few others disappeared. I asked the sergeant where they had gone.

"RTU cases, the lot of them," he replied. "That stands for Return To Unit. They've been sent back to their regiments as private soldiers, considered unsuitable as officer material. Ask yourself this – if you were a squaddie, what would you think if your officer went whining on because he was cold, wet and hungry all the time? That reminds me, Mr Pope, sir, there was a spot of blanco powder on one of your belt buckles at inspection this morning – so sharpen up or you'll be following them!"

After that, the dreaded letters RTU haunted all our waking hours. Next to go were those who were inclined to panic, followed by those who seemed indecisive. I could understand that, too, as we had been taught that sometimes our decisions would have to be made quickly in difficult and dangerous circumstances. After that, some who were unable to master important subjects also left.

By the middle of March 1943 the numbers on the course had shrunk to a hard core. There had been no departures for a while and we were told that we could order our officers' service dress uniform from the tailors. We were warned that this would be entirely at our own risk as the course had four weeks to run and any slackness would still result in our being returned to our units. As a result we tried all the harder.

During our passing-out parade we were inspected by a general who made a speech and then took the salute as we marched off the square. It had been hard work but we were now second lieutenants and felt a real sense of achievement. As I had requested, I was posted to the 4th Battalion, The Branchester Regiment, but given a week's leave before I had to report. I felt highly conspicuous in my service dress, shiny Sam Browne cross-belt and peaked cap and was genuinely surprised when I was saluted for the first time. Father looked me over, grunted his approval and said, "Well done!" Mother refused to let me change into comfortable civilian clothes and, although she had not been at all keen on my joining up, kept inviting her friends round to see her soldier son, which made me cringe with embarrassment.

By now, the news from the various war fronts was even better. In Tunisia the Germans and their allies, the Italians, had been penned into a narrow coastal strip. One evening during my leave, while we were sitting listening to the Nine o'Clock News on the radio, the announcer described how the Russians were liberating huge areas of their country.

"Hmm, there'll be no stopping them now," said Father, thoughtfully. "It will take time, but Stalin has mobilized millions of men. Hitler made a big mistake when he invaded Russia. Napoleon tried it and came to grief, and he was a lot brighter than Hitler."

"D'you think it will all be over before I get a chance to do any fighting?" I asked, having very mixed feelings on the subject. Part of me badly wanted to do my bit in bringing the War to a successful end, but part told me that, the risks of death or serious injury apart, active service would, at best, be most unpleasant.

"Don't be in such a hurry," he replied. "There's a long way to go yet. We have France, Belgium and the rest to liberate yet. Jerry's a good soldier and he won't make it easy for us."

He lapsed into silence for a while.

"I don't know how you'll find it, Andy," he said at length, "but my experience of war is that it's ninety per cent boredom and ten per cent sheer naked terror."

April 1943

The board outside Temple Marton camp gates read *4th Battalion The Branchester Regiment* and showed the regimental badge, a crowned dragon inside a laurel wreath, surrounded by battle honours inscribed on scrolls. The sentry directed me to Battalion Headquarters, where I reported to the adjutant, Captain Henry Dodsworth. I handed over my documents, which he glanced at briefly.

"Ah, yes, you're expected," he said. "I'll take you in to see the Colonel. I'm afraid he can't spare you much time as he only took over yesterday."

He knocked on the connecting door to the next office and opened it.

"Mr Pope, Colonel," he said, ushering me in. I saluted and was confronted by a stocky, muscular man whose battledress blouse bore the ribbons of the Distinguished Service Order and the North African campaign. A nameplate on his desk said Lieutenant Colonel JC Armitage, DSO. He rose to shake my hand.

"Glad to have you with us," he said. "Andrew, isn't it?

"It's Andy, usually, Colonel," I replied.

"Right. Just out of OCTU, I believe. Well, whatever they taught you there, I like things done my way, because it produces results, got it?"

"Yes, Colonel."

He stared at me intently, as though he had just spotted something.

"How old are you, Andy?"

"Eighteen, Colonel."

"Hmm. Well, just the same, I'm giving you Number Three Platoon in A Company. I'm trusting you to do a good job with it."

"Yes, Colonel."

"That will be all, Andy," said the adjutant.

I saluted again and followed him back to his office.

"You'd better get along to A Company HQ," he said. "Let them know you've arrived. Nigel Wood is acting as company commander for the moment."

Captain Nigel Wood was tall, fair-haired and genial. He made me feel welcome at once. He was about ten years older than me and told me that his family farmed near Branchester. He had joined the battalion as a Territorial in 1938.

"Mind you, there's only about half the original members

left," he said. "A lot were sent as reinforcements to the regiment's battalions overseas. Again, some of the older officers and Non Commissioned Officers (NCO) were no longer fit enough for an infantryman's war, so they were sent to less demanding jobs like training depots and guarding prisoners of war. They've been replaced by chaps from all over the country. You'll find that they're a good lot."

"What happened to my predecessor?" I asked.

"He's gone to the 1st Battalion. Should be joining them in Tunisia about now."

At that point the door opened and two cheerful-looking lieutenants strolled in.

"Spot of lunch, Nige, old bean?" asked one.

"I'll thank you to show your acting company commander some respect," replied Nigel, who did not seem in the least put out. He introduced them as John Crane and Tony Walters, who commanded, respectively, Numbers One and Two Platoons. John was tall, dark and wore a constant half-smile, while Tony was shorter and had a mass of curly fair hair.

"John is going to be our first casualty," said Tony, amiably. "You see, whatever we're doing, the CO (the battalion's Commanding Officer) picks A Company first, and the company commander picks One Platoon. Stands to reason, doesn't it?"

"Pay no attention to him," replied John. "He lives in a

world of his own. Always late for everything – if he ever finds a girl willing to marry him, she'll have gone off with someone else by the time he gets to the church!"

"By the way, how old are you, Andy?" asked Nigel.

"I'm eighteen."

"I was eighteen once," mused John.

"Surprised you can remember that far back," commented Tony, then turned confidentially to me. "He's twenty-four, you know. And as for Nigel, no one has ever found out how old he is. Could even be thirty!"

"Your platoon sergeant, Sergeant Warriner, will meet you in the company office at two o'clock, Andy," said Nigel during lunch. "He's mustard – regular soldier, wounded serving with the 5th Battalion at Alamein. You're lucky to have him."

It was clear from the moment I set eyes on him that Sergeant Albert Warriner was a highly professional, no-nonsense sort of NCO. His turnout was immaculate, from his gleaming cap badge to his shining boots. His tunic bore the Military Medal and North African Campaign medals. Of middle height, he gave the impression of lean, muscular hardness. His sandy hair was brushed back. His angular face contained a long nose above a rat-trap mouth. His eyes were level, shrewd and never seemed to blink. I had the impression that he had summed me up at a glance. He could have been any age between thirty and forty. When he spoke it was in short bursts, with an edge of menace in his voice. He threw up a salute that quivered with precision.

"Mr Pope, sir?" he said. "I'm Sergeant Warriner. You're taking over Number 3 Platoon, I believe."

"That's right," I replied, returning the salute and shaking hands.

"Let's take a turn round the camp, sir. Show you what's what."

It sounded more like an order than a suggestion. We left the office and talked as he indicated what the various buildings were used for. When I asked him about himself he said that he had been in the Army for fifteen years, was married and had a family.

"I understand that you were wounded at Alamein," I said. "And I see that you've been awarded the Military Medal."

"Ha!" His face remained completely expressionless when he laughed. "Ha! Ha! Shouldn't wonder if they had one spare and decided I needed it, sir! There's better men deserved it and didn't get it. Now, how about you, sir? Just out of OCTU, I'm told. How old would that make you?"

When I told him, his only acknowledgement was a small upwards nod which could have meant either

17

that he disapproved or simply that he had absorbed the fact.

"You'll be inspecting the Platoon at morning parade tomorrow, sir?" he said at length.

"Yes, Sergeant, and after Colonel Armitage has addressed the battalion I'd like to see them one at a time in the platoon office."

"Very good, sir. I'll set them to weapon cleaning while that's going on."

I suddenly found myself at a loss for what to say next. A hint of a friendly smile appeared at the corners of his mouth.

"Difficult time for you, this, sir. Just remember – you command the Platoon and I run it for you. If you need advice, just ask. All my young officers have turned out well, I'm glad to say. You'll be all right."

"Thank you, Sergeant. I appreciate what you say."

I felt a great sense of relief, knowing that I would have the backing of such an experienced man.

"There's four Fs you must remember when dealing with the men," he continued. "Be Fair, Firm and Friendly, but never Familiar. Now, if you'll excuse me, I've things to attend to, so I'll see you on morning parade, sir."

He saluted and marched away smartly.

I spent the rest of the afternoon settling in. It had alarmed me that I had been asked how old I was so often. I looked in the mirror. Aware that I did indeed appear young for my age, I wondered what the Platoon would think about being commanded by me.

At morning parade next day the order was given for platoon commanders to inspect their men. As I walked towards Number Three Platoon, Sergeant Warriner marched forward to meet me, halted with a crash of boots and saluted.

"Number Three Platoon ready for your inspection, sir!"

"Thank you, Sergeant Warriner."

I was conscious that over thirty pairs of eyes were watching me curiously. Sergeant Warriner fell in beside me as I walked towards the ranks.

"Take longer than you usually would to inspect each man, sir," he said in an undertone. "They're sizing you up, so let 'em know you're sizing them up, too. And remember – praise where it's due, blame where it isn't."

Halfway along the front rank I stopped in front of a large man with a broken nose. His boots shone, his belt buckles and cap badge gleamed and his trouser creases were sharp.

"Name?"

"Baker, sir."

"A good turnout, Baker. Well done."

"Sir."

So far so good, but in the rear rank I came across a man

whose turnout was passable but whose chin was covered in stubble. Instead of staring straight ahead, he regarded me with something like a contemptuous leer.

"Name?"

"Grover, sir."

"Why haven't you shaved this morning?"

"I have, sir."

"You have not. Why not?"

"I have, sir. Must have used an old blade. If you shave you'll know you can't get new ones often, 'cos there's a war on, sir."

He was, in fact, suggesting that I was a boy who was too young to shave and therefore unfit to give orders to older men like him. I had been warned that, sooner or later, someone would challenge my authority, but I had not expected that it would happen so soon. I was horribly nervous but knew that I must win this confrontation if I was to establish myself as the platoon commander. His leer became wider and more self-confident. I was suddenly very angry and surprised myself with my response.

"When I want a lecture on current affairs from you I'll ask for it, Grover! Appear in front of me again like that and you're in for serious trouble – and you can cut out the dumb insolence, too!"

"Charge him, sir?" asked Sergeant Warriner.

A formal disciplinary charge would mean that Grover

would be marched in front of Nigel Wood, who would sentence him to be confined to barracks for a period, a punishment known to the soldiers as "jankers". This involved performing numerous extra fatigue duties and parading at the Guard Room at various times in full equipment. However, I had dealt with the incident and did not want to exaggerate its importance.

"No, not this time, but he's had the only chance he's getting. Find him some extra duties."

"Be a pleasure, sir. Grover – report to the Provost Sergeant after tea tonight. He wants the grass round the Guard Room cutting. Should take you about three hours if you're lucky."

"Yes, Sergeant," replied Grover, his face sullen and resentful.

After the inspection we were to be addressed by Colonel Armitage. I ordered Sergeant Warriner to march the Platoon to the camp cinema and made my own way there. When the whole battalion was assembled the officers filed into the front row of seats. As Colonel Armitage began to walk down the aisle, followed by the adjutant, everyone was called to attention by Mr Ash, the red-faced, fiercely moustached Regimental Sergeant Major (RSM). The Colonel mounted the stage, motioning us to sit down.

"Since 1940 this battalion has been engaged on anti-invasion duties here in East Anglia," he said. "That was a necessary job. It was also a boring job, and now that Hitler

21

is firmly on the defensive and there is no prospect of our country being invaded, the job has come to an end. You will no doubt have wished at times that you could be playing a more active role in the War, because everyone knows that until the enemy has been beaten none of us will be going home. Well, the moment for you to play that role has now come."

You could have heard a pin drop in the short pause that followed.

"My task is to turn you into a fit, efficient, hard-fighting battalion, ready to take the field. I can tell you that something very big indeed is being planned. I do not know what, when or where it is to take place because I have not been told myself, but I have been told that you will be a part of it. Now, some of you will have made yourselves very comfortable here over the years. I can promise you that you will find the next few months very uncomfortable, but at the end of it you will be leaner, harder and capable of tackling the toughest of enemies."

He paused again to let this sink in.

"No one will be excused. Not even the clerks, storemen, batmen, cooks and the others who somehow manage to stay out of the rain when the rest of us are getting soaked!"

There was much laughter at this.

"That's all I have to say for the present. Carry on, please, Mr Ash."

The RSM called the battalion to attention and we filed out of the cinema.

It took the rest of the morning and the whole of the afternoon to complete my interviews with the Platoon, during which Sergeant Warriner stood behind me. I recorded the personal details of my men in a notebook. These included their home town, their civilian occupation, whether they were married and had families of their own, their hobbies, sports and interests. I also asked them whether they had any personal problems.

I saw the junior NCO first. The three section commanders, Corporals Gray, Morris and Sherwood, had been in the Territorial Army before the War. In civilian life, they had been, respectively, a plasterer, a milkman and a refuse collector. They were all married and seemed solid and reliable. The Lance Corporals were newer arrivals but showed promise. I then saw each of the privates. The Platoon had its characters and it was them who interested me most. Grover I had already encountered. Now properly shaven, he glared resentfully at me. He said he was an orphan, had no fixed address and had worked as a casual labourer since he left school at twelve. He had no interest in sport, or anything else for that matter. His record revealed a string of civilian convictions for petty theft, brawling and drunkenness.

His military charge sheet contained a long list of offences, including insolence, insubordination, failure to obey orders, and many more.

"Why don't you sort yourself out?" I asked.

"Not my fault, sir," he replied, glowering at Sergeant Warriner. "They've got it in for me, the lot of them."

I asked him why and he simply shrugged. When I asked him if he had any particular problems he gave vent to a sudden flash of anger.

"Oh, yes, I got a problem, sir. My problem is the whole piggin' Army! Why should I fight for my country? What's the country ever done for me? This war's nothin' to me."

"Want a reason, do you?" shouted Sergeant Warriner. I thought he would explode with fury. "Then think of the innocent women and children killed in the Blitz! And there'll be more before this lot's over. You'll fight for your country and like it, like the rest of us! Now get out of my sight!"

"I'm sorry about that, sir," he said when Grover had gone. "He's a bad 'un. He'll be over the wall at the first sign of trouble, mark my words."

"Can we get rid of him?"

"Ha! Don't think I haven't tried. Easier said than done, sir, because no one wants him."

"Isn't he a bad influence on the rest of the Platoon?"

"They ignore him, sir. Weighed him up as soon as

he arrived. Can't name one of them you could say was his friend."

"I'm not surprised. Seems to hate everyone, including himself. Can we make anything out of him, d'you think?"

"I've met his type before, sir. Sometimes they'll surprise you and buckle-to when the going's rough, but don't count on it in this case."

Then there was Baker. He was married with two boys, had been a coalman, and was an amateur middleweight boxer who, because he was light on his feet, had also won ballroom-dancing contests. He gave every appearance of being a good soldier, but his crimesheet showed that he had been punished regularly for going absent without leave.

"Why?" I asked him.

"Personal reasons, sir."

"If you've got a problem then tell the platoon commander," said Sergeant Warriner. "But for this you could have had a stripe on your arm, maybe two."

"Prefer not to say, Sar'nt."

"Pity," Sergeant Warriner said when Baker had gone. "Ten to one it's wife trouble. Corporal Gray knows, I'm sure of it, but I can't get it out of him."

Private Joseph Haggerty was Irish and came from Liverpool. He was short, dark, had a shifty expression, but was good humoured and played football for the battalion.

He described his civilian occupation as general dealer. I asked him what he dealt in.

"Oh, whatever comes me way, sir," he replied, grinning broadly. "I'll sell it on, like, for the best price I can get."

"He means he's a burglar, sir," commented Sergeant Warriner.

"Ay, come on, Sarge!" protested Haggerty. "Yer know I don't nick off me mates! I've gone straight since I joined up."

"Keep it that way!" snapped the Sergeant.

Haggerty leaned confidentially towards me, smiling like a conspirator and tapping the side of his nose.

"Mind you, sir, if ever yer need anythin', like nylon stockings an' such as are in short supply, I do know a coupla helpful fellers."

"That will be all, Haggerty," I said.

Private Adrian Helsby-Frodsham was about thirty, of sturdy build and dapper appearance with a gold watch chain stretching between the pockets of his battledress tunic.

"How do you do?" he said in a cultured voice.

"Never mind how d'you damn well do!" bellowed Sergeant Warriner. "It's your platoon commander you're talking to! And get rid of that watch chain – I've told you about that before! This is your signaller, sir, when he's not putting on his Posh Charlie act."

"I see from your documents that you were an artist in civilian life," I said.

"Oh, I do the odd dawb, sir," he replied. "Portraits mostly – keeps the old body and soul joined together, what?"

"And what are your interests?"

"Principally, painting the pretty wives of rich men, sir. That's rather rewarding. Then there's fast cars, good food and wine and the occasional holiday in France. Simple things, really."

"I don't know, of course, but it's possible we might all be taking a trip to France. Can you speak French?"

"Yes, I studied in Paris for three years, so I'm reasonably fluent."

It occurred to me that he could be a useful member of the Platoon in a variety of ways.

"Can you draw cartoons?" I asked.

"I can, sir – lots of good subjects hereabouts," he replied, looking pointedly at Sergeant Warriner, who responded with a stony stare.

"Perhaps you could do some of the Platoon," I suggested. "You know what I mean – the things that happen while we're training and so on. We can put them on the notice board for a week, then keep them in a platoon scrapbook."

He agreed, and Sergeant Warriner clearly approved of

the idea, commenting that it would do some people good to see themselves as others saw them.

Last to appear was my batman – that is, soldier servant – who also acted as my runner in the field. Private Timothy Allen, whom I had already met briefly in the Mess, had been a valet at the Savoy Hotel in London and it was natural that a former commander of the battalion had initially taken him as his batman. However, Allen could not stop talking about the royalty, aristocrats, admirals, generals, film stars and politicians whom he had looked after at the hotel, driving everyone to distraction. He had therefore slid down the battalion's hierarchy, through the majors, captains and senior lieutenants, and as I was the most junior officer for the present I was landed with him.

"I imagine that you find the Army very different from your earlier occupation," I said, and instantly regretted it.

"Oh, yes, sir," he replied. "It's not that I don't approve of the War or the Army, sir, because I believe we're right to fight against Hitler – he and his crowd were never gentlemen, sir, so the dreadful things they've done came as no surprise to me. That's why I joined up. No, sir, the main difference is financial, you see. Many of the people I looked after at the hotel were generous, sir, very generous. Now take Mr Niven, sir – Mr David Niven, the actor, that is. . ."

"Stop talkin'!" snapped Sergeant Warriner.

"You know that your duties involve digging a slit trench for us both, don't you?" I asked.

"Indeed I do, sir. I dig a very fine slit trench, even if I do say so myself. Apart from the two of us, I'm always very fussy who I invite into it. After all, one wouldn't invite just anyone into one's home, would one? I like to keep up standards, sir, even in the field. There are some people. . ."

I could see Sergeant Warriner raising his eyes to heaven in despair.

"Thank you, Allen, that's all," I said, but he continued talking as he made his way to the door.

"Oh, by the way, sir, I've buffed up the buttons on your service dress, creased your trousers, and polished your Sam Browne belt and shoes. And as soon as you're back, sir, I think I'd better give those boots you're wearing a bit of attention. And you'll need more handkerchiefs, sir. I like my gentleman to have a clean handkerchief every day, and you've less than a week's supply left. . ."

There was a sense of deep and enjoyable silence after he had gone.

"Well, that's that," I said, closing my notebook.

"Mixed bunch – is that what you're thinking, sir?" asked Sergeant Warriner. "They rub along together pretty well, considering. Handled right, they won't let you down."

Just then the door opened and Nigel poked his head round.

"Spot o' news, Andy," he said. "The new company commander arrives next Monday. Name's Duncan Flint, Distinguished Service Order and Military Cross, no less. Bit of a hot shot by all accounts."

"Ha!" Sergeant Warriner gave one of his mirthless laughs. "Knew him pre-war. When the 2nd Battalion was forced to surrender at Tobruk last year, he refused to give up until Jerry promised his company the Honours of War. Then he escaped from a prisoner-of-war train in Italy and made it home. No disrespect intended, gentlemen, but he'll make you earn every penny of your pay. You may even hate his guts at the end of it, but we'll have a damn fine company!"

April – September 1943

The following Monday I was conducting a map-reading class when Company Sergeant Major Darracott appeared.

"Sorry to interrupt, sir, but Major Flint, the new company commander, has arrived," he said. "He'd like to see you in his office at 11:00 prompt."

I reached the office at the same time as John. We strolled in and saluted the figure seated behind the desk. He was looking down at some papers, so all that I could see was that he was well-built and had iron-grey hair. Nigel stood behind him, looking ill at ease. I could hear Tony's feet hurrying along the corridor. He entered the room and saluted. Only then did the man at the desk look up. He had a clipped moustache and the most piercing eyes I have ever seen.

"Get out and come in again – all of you!" he snarled. There was a frightening edge to his voice. We did as we were bidden, halted in front of his desk and saluted together. He regarded each of us minutely in turn.

"Now let us get one thing straight from the start," he said. "When I say eleven-hundred hours, I mean precisely that. It is now thirty seconds past eleven and I regard that as being very late indeed. If you are thirty seconds late attacking after the barrage has lifted you will have given the enemy time to man his machine-guns and you will lose a lot of men. Do you agree, gentlemen?"

"Yes, sir," we said in chorus.

"Good. I also want you to know that I regard any hesitation or surliness in carrying out an order as disobedience, that half-hearted effort is a sign of laziness and that if you knowingly communicate inaccurate or incomplete information to me that is the equivalent of lying. Do we understand each other?"

"Yes, sir," we said again.

"I am glad that is clear. I shall require the pleasure of your company for a drink after dinner, gentlemen. You may now return to your duties."

We saluted, turned about and left the office.

"Phew!" said Tony. "I think I've just been run over by a steamroller!"

Dinner in the Mess was usually a pleasant, relaxed affair, but on this occasion Nigel, John, Tony and I were more concerned with what lay in store for us than with what we were eating. Later, when we had settled ourselves in armchairs in the ante-room, Major Flint joined us and instructed one of the Mess staff to bring us drinks from the bar. It was soon apparent that this was not a friendly gesture, but one made for the same reasons

I had interviewed everyone in my platoon. He asked each of us a series of searching questions and was obviously making up his mind about us. As our interrogation drew to an end, Nigel asked him about the fall of Tobruk.

"Yes, I thought that would come up, so I'll tell you now and get it out of the way," he said. "We had no tanks left and when Jerry broke through the defences and reached the town, the general in command, a South African named Klopper, didn't have much choice other than to surrender. Our battalion was holding an area of the eastern defences, near the sea. With Jerry tanks crawling all over them, the rest of the battalion obeyed the order to surrender. I didn't, because my company was lucky enough to be holding a position between two wadis, that is, steep-sided, dried-up river courses, with a cliff covering our rear. The only way Jerry could get at us was across a stretch of ground between the wadis, and I had covered that with a minefield. At the time I believed that the Eighth Army wouldn't stand for the loss of Tobruk and would counter-attack, so all we had to do was hold out until they arrived. What I didn't know was that the Army had taken a real beating and was retreating across the frontier into Egypt."

He paused for a moment, remembering what had happened.

"Well, we held 'em off for two days," he continued. "They lost three tanks on the minefield, and the rest couldn't get past them. They shelled us time and again, but we beat them off every time their infantry attacked and caused them a lot of grief. We also lost a lot of good men. By the morning of the third day the company was down to the size of a platoon. The riflemen had about five rounds left apiece, and the Bren gunners less than a magazine. We had no food and what water was left we saved for the wounded. Anyway, a Jerry colonel appeared with a flag of truce. He said we'd put up a terrific fight but if we didn't surrender he had orders to exterminate us. I told him that if he tried that every one of us would take two or three of his men with us. I knew it was hopeless, so I said that I would surrender on two conditions – first, that he granted us the Honours of War, and second, that he arranged for our wounded to be attended to immediately. He was a decent enough sort and agreed.

"We spent the morning smartening up and making the wounded as comfortable as possible. At noon, the agreed time, I led what was left of the company through a gap in the minefield. Then we formed up, fixed bayonets, and marched between two lines of Jerries. They presented arms and their officers saluted. When we halted I thanked the men for all they had done and ordered them to ground arms. I watched them being marched off under guard. That was the worst day of my life and I have no intention of repeating it."

We all sat silent for a moment. I think we were all a little surprised that he had cared so much about his men.

"You managed to escape, though, sir," said Tony, breaking the silence.

"Yes. I was flown to Italy and held in an Italian prisoner-of-war camp until August. The guards were a sloppy lot and I managed to pinch a tyre lever when one of them was working on his lorry. I suppose I thought it would come in handy as a cosh. Anyway, it was decided that the British officers would be sent to Germany and we were put aboard a train consisting of cattle trucks. I began working on the truck's floorboards with the tyre lever. I got one up, then more, until I had made a hole big enough for me to drop through on to the track. I could see through the ventilation slits in the side of the truck that we were getting closer to the Alps. The train made frequent stops, but I decided to wait until it was dark and we were in open country. The right moment seemed to arrive and I dropped through. I think others would have followed, but just then the train began to move again. Maybe some of them tried it later. Anyway, I lay between the rails until the train was out of sight."

"What happened next, sir?" I asked.

"I became a thief. At various times I stole bicycles, clothes, food and money. By moving only at night and staying hidden during the day, I somehow got over the mountains into France. The Jerries weren't occupying the south of the country at that time, but the French government, located in a town called Vichy, were collaborating with them and would have handed me over like a shot if their police had got their hands on me. I was sitting in a café in Nice, looking like a scarecrow, when two characters put a revolver in my back and marched me down an alley and into a house. They belonged to the Resistance, and while they suspected that I was an escaped British POW, they were worried that I might be a German posing as one. So, for the next three days I was grilled over and over again. At length London confirmed my details over their short-wave radio link. From that point on, it was plain sailing. I was spirited across southern France to the Pyrenees, where I was handed over to the group's Spanish friends. They had been on the losing side during the Spanish Civil War and they had no love for General Franco, who, as you know, is one of Hitler's best pals. To cut a long story short, I was taken through some pretty remote areas of Spain until we reached the frontier with Gibraltar. I was taken across in a coffin in the back of a hearse. Pretty creepy, I can tell you. In Gibraltar they found a space for me in a homeward-bound destroyer."

We had all listened in silent wonder and admiration as Duncan Flint told his story. Suddenly, he stood up and his manner changed abruptly.

"I'll wish you good night, gentlemen. I shall be joining you for a run at 06:00."

"Er, you remember you've ordered a company run for 08:00?" asked Nigel, startled.

"Quite right – you should be nicely warmed up by then!" was the reply.

It soon became clear that Major Flint intended sparing his officers nothing. At the morning parade following the company run he addressed everyone.

"It won't be too long now before we find ourselves on active service. I intend working you hard, but no harder than I work myself and your officers. We have a heavy programme of exercises ahead of us. During those exercises I shall sometimes tell platoon commanders or their sergeants that they have been 'killed'. That will mean that corporals may find themselves commanding their platoons for part of an exercise. Likewise, lance corporals may find themselves acting as platoon sergeants and private soldiers commanding sections. Why are we doing this? Because I intend encouraging you to use your personal initiative. It has been my experience that soldiers who use their initiative survive, and those who don't, don't."

He now had everyone's undivided attention. I exchanged glances with Nigel, John and Tony. It was apparent that none of us had expected this.

"I want you to remember a few things at all times, no matter how tired you are," the Major continued. "Always expect the unexpected. Think of everything the enemy might possibly do, then it's no surprise when he does it. Treat him to a dose of the unexpected, because he doesn't like it. If you are in contact with him, never move without covering fire if you can avoid it. Learn what you can about the enemy's weapons – you may have to use 'em in a tight spot. And if that spot is so tight that you think things couldn't get worse, keep giving the enemy a hard time. You'll be surprised what you can get away with."

Duncan Flint certainly kept his promise. There were early morning runs three times a week and we were sent over the assault course whenever there was a spare moment. Fortunately, I was still as fit as I had been at OCTU and didn't experience too much difficulty, but many of the others found it hard going until they toughened up. Then there were platoon, company and battalion exercises, sometimes carried out in company with tanks. These included attacks, occupying a defensive position, withdrawals, street fighting in a dummy village, and patrolling at night. During these, the "enemy" consisted of one or other of our brigade's battalions. As we progressed, a friendly rivalry began to develop between A Company's three platoons. Colonel Armitage and Major Flint, who both had personal experience of war, could often be seen arguing fiercely with the exercise umpires and directing staff, who had not. This caused Sergeant Warriner much wry amusement.

"Ha! They're supposed to teach us," he said. "Now we end up teaching them! All they know is what they read in tactical manuals!"

I knew what he meant because Warriner's practical experience had become evident on the first day of the exercises. I had turned up with my issue map case and binoculars slung round my neck.

"Looks as though I'll be needing a new officer ten minutes after we go into action, sir," he remarked after giving me a cursory glance.

"What do you mean, Sergeant?"

"Your map case, sir. Reflects in the sun. Jerry sniper spots it, takes a look through his telescopic sight, sees that you're wearing binoculars. Puts two and two together – map case plus binoculars means you're someone important. Draws a bead on you and the platoon has lost its officer. My advice is ditch the map case, keep the map in your trouser-leg pocket and tuck your binoculars into your battledress tunic."

I did as he suggested. A few minutes later Major Flint walked over.

"I see you've been taking survival lessons, Andy – well done," he said, and nodded approvingly at Sergeant Warriner.

In fact, this was one of the few occasions on which I received any praise. When I did well I was called Andy, but

I seemed to make one mistake after another and so most of the time it was Mr Pope.

"Mr Pope," the Major would say, "your two leading sections came over that crest like a line of tin ducks at a shooting gallery! Learn to use the ground as cover, for God's sake!"

Or, "Mr Pope, you failed to identify that machine gun post to your left. You and your platoon headquarters have been wiped out!"

Or, worst of all, the dreaded phrase, "See if you can get it right this time, boy!"

To be fair, the Major always made these comments out of the men's hearing and explained the nature of the mistakes to the Platoon in a general way so that they would learn not to make them themselves. He also encouraged us platoon commanders to be more flexible in our approach to tactical problems.

"You have got to win the fire-fight before you even think of attacking," he said. "The German light machine gun, the Spandau or MG34, is a belt-fed weapon theoretically capable of firing over 800 rounds per minute. Your Brens, on the other hand, are magazine-fed and can only produce a theoretical 450 rounds a minute. So concentrate *all* your Brens into a single fire base and take out his MG34s one at a time. You'll find that once his machine-gunners have gone, the average Jerry rifleman tends to give up."

Likewise, he had his own ideas about using the PIAT (Projector Infantry Anti-Tank), which launched a hollow-charge bomb capable of penetrating a tank's armour, three of which were issued to each company.

"Don't think you have to wait for a tank to use your PIAT," he told us. "If the enemy's holed up in a house, use it to bring it down round his ears."

Tactics such as these, based on his own experience, were to prove invaluable when the time came for action. Even so, there were days when I hated him, and I know that Nigel, John and Tony felt the same. The odd thing was, Duncan Flint had an uncanny ability to read my thoughts, which I found disturbing. When, without saying a word, I had decided to do something, he would suddenly bark at me to do exactly what I had intended. This happened quite a lot and was very annoying. Once, after he had given me a real dressing down, I was glaring with dislike at his retreating back when he unexpectedly halted, wheeled round and fixed me with his terrifying stare.

"I don't give a damn what you think, laddie!" he snarled. "Now, let's get one thing straight, shall we? My intention is that one day this company will earn a name for itself in history, as did my last company – and you're part of it, whether you like it or not! Have you got that?"

"Yes, sir," I replied, somewhat shaken. This was just what

he might have said if he had known what I was thinking about him, which was far from pleasant.

My father had told me that a young officer's education is completed in the Sergeants' Mess, as the sergeants' long service has given them a wide understanding of human nature. It was the custom for the orderly officer of the day (a junior officer who was responsible for mounting the camp's Guard which provided sentries during the night, inspecting the cookhouse and many other things) to be invited into the Sergeants' Mess after his ten o'clock inspection of the Guard. On one such occasion, after paying my respects to Mr Ash, I found myself sitting on a bar stool between Company Sergeant Major Darracott and Sergeant Warriner.

"Bit of a hard time for you, just now, sir," said the Sergeant Major, who was a Dunkirk veteran.

"Well, if there's a way of doing things wrong, I usually find it, don't I, Sergeant Major?" I replied ruefully.

They both laughed.

"Don't let it get you down, sir," said Sergeant Warriner. "We've all of us had bad patches at one time or another. They come to an end."

"Maybe you'd be surprised to know that during the exercises there wasn't a platoon leader in the battalion who didn't get strips torn off him by his company commander or even the Colonel, sir," added the Sergeant Major. "True, Major Flint is taking more trouble with you, but he wouldn't be wasting his time if he thought you were useless, would he? You'd have been long gone to some depot for the unwanted."

"Maybe you're right," I said, feeling somewhat reassured. "I dare say I'll get used to him in time."

They exchanged knowing glances.

"Fact is, sir, the Major's seen more than his fair share of scrapping in this war," said Sergeant Warriner. "Seen most of his old friends killed or badly wounded. That hurts – I know because I've had some."

"What we're saying is this," continued the Sergeant Major. "Friends are for peacetime. Being friendly is the way to make friends – he doesn't want 'em, so he isn't. That doesn't stop him being a damn fine officer. D'you get my drift, sir?"

"Yes, I think so," I said. "I'll bear in mind what you say, and thanks for the advice."

I felt much better after this. At first, my handling of my platoon during the exercises had been stiff and awkward, and the men sensed it. However, as my confidence grew they became used to me and we began to work as a team. Grover continued to give trouble in a minor sort of way but was under control. Baker, however, went absent without leave once more. On his return he offered no excuse and was sentenced to fourteen days confined to barracks. I warned him that if he committed the offence again he would probably be sent for a spell in a detention barracks.

Curiously, it was Baker who was responsible for my getting to know the men better. During the inter-company boxing contest, A Company was level-pegging with D Company. Everything depended on the last match, in which Baker was fighting. He had the measure of his opponent from the start, but during the last round a strange look came over his face and he continued raining blows on him after the bell had rung. After he was pulled off he seemed to come to, went across and apologized to the other man, saying that he didn't know what had come over him. Needless to say, he was disqualified and we lost the match. Major Flint had wanted A Company to win and he was furious.

"Baker is *your* man," he snapped at me as he stalked out of the gymnasium. "Sort him out!"

Sergeant Warriner had said that Corporal Gray knew what was troubling Baker, but when I approached him he was reluctant to discuss the matter. I said that it was in Baker's interest that he should, because if Baker went absent without leave again he would be sentenced to detention. That meant his pay would be stopped and his wife and family would suffer because of it. He thought about it for a minute, then told me the story.

"Ron Baker and I have been friends for years, sir," he said. "Well, one night before the War we were at a dance. That's where he met Mary. Well, being a boxer, Ron's light on his feet and a good dancer. The two of them won plenty of competitions. They got married and now they've got two boys. Ron thinks the world of them. Well, just after the War started, Mary fell ill. She's never really recovered and if anything she's got worse. Her doctor says an operation would set her right, but every penny they've got goes to paying his bills, buying medicine and looking after the boys. There's nothing left to pay for the operation, nor will there ever be on a private's pay. Ron's worried sick about it, and that's why he keeps going absent without leave. What makes it worse, sir, is that he's a proud man who won't take charity from anyone."

"Thank you, Corporal, I'll see what we can do," I replied. "In the meantime, don't mention any of this to Baker."

I reported this to Duncan Flint and together we went to see Colonel Armitage.

"You say that in every other respect Baker is a good soldier with the potential to become an NCO?" asked the Colonel after he had considered the problem.

"Yes, Colonel," I said. "If we can't help he'll keep going absent without leave. He knows he'll get detention next time, but it won't stop him, and nobody will be any better off."

"I will support that, Colonel," added Duncan Flint.

"Quite so," said the Colonel. "Andy, find out who is the family doctor, will you? While you're doing that, I'll talk to the Secretary of the Regimental Benevolent Fund."

Corporal Gray gave me the doctor's name, which I passed on. A couple of days later I was called into Duncan Flint's office.

"Your man Baker," he said. "The Secretary of the Benevolent Fund has spoken to his doctor. He, in turn, has spoken to the specialist who will carry out the operation. In the circumstances, the specialist will reduce his fee, which will be paid by the Fund. Nevertheless, I want you to verify Mrs Baker's situation for yourself. You can borrow my jeep on Sunday morning and drive over to see her – take Baker with you."

I told Corporal Gray that we might be making some progress, and that Baker should meet me at the Guard Room at 08:30 next Sunday, but not the reason why.

That Sunday, I found Baker waiting for me at the Guard Room, wearing a puzzled expression.

"Where are we going, sir?" he asked as we turned out the camp gates.

"What's your home address?" I asked.

"22 Webber Street, Donby, sir. Why?"

"Then that's where we're going."

"Someone's been talking," he said, his face flushing with anger. "I'll deal with him when I get back."

"No, you won't. He was thinking of your boys. He says they're proud of their dad – how d'you think they'd feel about you ending up in detention barracks and no money coming in?"

He remained silent, but I could see that he understood.

"And another thing," I added. "Your wife needs an operation – let's see if we can get her one, shall we? That way, she gets better, the boys get looked after, and you stay in the Platoon."

"I'll take charity from no man," he said stubbornly. "I've never had 'owt but what I've earned, fair and square."

"It's not charity. The Regiment looks after its own and the Benevolent Fund exists for just this sort of situation. Besides, I know you wouldn't want your wife to suffer longer than she had to, or become so ill that she couldn't look after the boys. Apart from which, we both know that if the War hadn't broken out, you'd have earned enough to deal with the problem yourself."

"Happen you're right, sir," he said with a sigh. "Seems I'd best put my pride in my pocket, then."

About an hour later we drove into the small industrial town in which he lived. He directed me into a street of terraced houses and asked me to pull up outside one of them. As he got out of the jeep two small boys who had been playing football ran towards him with delighted yells. When they had calmed down a little he brought them over.

"These are my lads, sir. This is Jack, he's nearly seven, and this is Tom, he's five. This is Mr Pope, boys – he's my officer, so mind your manners, the pair of you. I'll just let your mam know we're here."

"Hello," I said. "Ever sat in a jeep before? Jump in."

A few minutes later I joined Baker in the house and was introduced to his wife. She would have been good-looking but for an expression of pain that had become etched on her face, and she moved slowly and with difficulty. It seemed obvious to me that she couldn't go on much longer like that. I told her what had been decided and that she should contact her doctor, who would arrange for the specialist to carry out the operation.

"I don't know what to say, sir," she said, and burst into tears. Nothing in my training had prepared me for this and I was horribly embarrassed.

"Just get well, that's what we all want," I mumbled, and told Baker I would wait for him in the jeep outside.

"You've taken a ton weight off my shoulders, sir," he said when I dropped him off at the Guard Room. "Thanks – we're both very grateful to you."

It was now approaching lunchtime. I found Duncan Flint reading a newspaper in the ante-room. He barely glanced up when I told him the result of my visit.

"Good," he said at length, turning a page. "If there are any more personal problems in Three Platoon, see that you sort them out before they become this serious."

He was right, of course, but his manner infuriated me. The following week Mrs Baker had her operation and made a good recovery. After that more of the men came to me with their problems. I found myself arguing with Duncan Flint about their leave entitlement, with the Paymaster about their pay and with the Quartermaster about their kit. I arranged compassionate leave when members of their families died and saw to it that they had legal advice when they needed it.

I had been advised that it was sometimes wise to be blind to minor faults and deaf to chance remarks that one might overhear. One day, however, I heard some of the men talking about me when they thought I was out of earshot.

"He's all right, is Mr Pope," said one.

I felt as though I had grown a foot in height.

October 1943 – May 1944

During the months that followed we still remained in ignorance about where we would be sent. Duncan Flint refused to speculate, but Nigel felt that because we trained a great deal with armoured regiments, it was unlikely to be Italy – the Italian campaign had become an infantry war in which tanks had only a limited role to play. More than ever, therefore, we became convinced that we were being trained for the invasion of France.

This seemed to be confirmed when, in October, each company was sent to the Battle School at Thetford. There, we carried out live ammunition exercises and completed a stiff assault course during which constant explosions simulated shellfire and machine guns fired inches above our heads as we crawled through or jumped over the numerous obstacles. I was extremely nervous, for I knew that people had been injured and even killed during this sort of training. Fortunately, nothing of that sort happened, and I suppose it gave us all an idea of what to expect. However, looking back, I now know that it could not possibly duplicate the sheer naked fear we experienced when we were faced with the real thing.

We were getting our breath back when Nigel pointed to a group of officers in unfamiliar uniforms talking to the Directing Staff.

"Americans," he said. "Come to see how it's done, I expect."

Being based in East Anglia we had met plenty of American airmen, but these were the first soldiers we had seen, although the United States had entered the War on the side of the Allies in December 1941.

"I like their waterproof uniforms," said John. "They call them combat fatigues, I believe. Those round helmets of theirs must be easier to keep on than the ones we've got – mine bounces all over the place."

"That's no surprise," commented Tony. "You've got a pointed skull like a Martian. Sometimes I think you are a Martian."

"Frankly, old chap, yours wouldn't stay on at all if you hadn't got so much hair," retorted John. "Better not visit the barber's – no one would recognize you when you came out!"

"Uh-oh! Looks as though we're getting a visitor," observed Nigel as Duncan Flint walked towards us with an American officer whose helmet had the single white star of a brigadier general on the front. The Sergeant Major called the company to attention and we officers saluted. The American was portly and wore rimless glasses. I thought he looked like a banker in a Hollywood film. A white identification label saying FASSBINDER was sewn on to his tunic.

"At ease, men," he said, grinning broadly. "I've been watching you this morning and I consider that you gave a fine display of fitness, speed, stamina and determination. I guess that you guys are just about combat ready."

The men were obviously pleased. Then, to my horror, Haggerty, the joker from Liverpool, spoke up.

"You goin' to have a go yourself, then, sir?"

Duncan Flint's eyes flicked angrily from Haggerty to me and I expected to be called to account later. Fortunately, the American took it in his stride.

"Hell, no, son," he replied, chuckling. "You fellers have been at this since the War began – we're just getting started! When the time comes, though, we'll be right in there pitching alongside you!"

When the American had gone, Duncan Flint turned to face the company, hands on hips. I think we all knew what to expect.

"Now I'll tell you what I think," he said. "By my standards you were satisfactory – just. I've seen you move much faster but the only reason I'm not sending you round again is that when you really come under fire you'll discover you have a turn of speed you never thought possible!"

The men laughed. I think they liked his style, which was more than we did at the time. Telling the Sergeant Major to dismiss the company, he turned to us.

"And as for you four, I expected more from you!" he snapped. "You should have set the pace, not conformed to it. You're paid to lead, so lead!"

"Miserable so-and-so!" muttered John angrily as the Major stalked off. "Nothing we do ever seems to satisfy him!"

I could see that Nigel was angry, too, but as the company's second-in-command he had a duty to support Duncan Flint, whatever he thought privately.

"He's doing his job as he thinks best," he said. "Remember, he's had a lot more experience than we have. What's more, though he's older than us, he still got round the course first, and that gives him the right to criticize."

"It wouldn't hurt him to say 'well done' now and again, would it?" I commented.

"You know, he's never said as much, but I think he's rather pleased at the way the company is coming on," Nigel replied. "Just the same, I don't think he'll let up until he's satisfied he can take us into action. That's when I think he'll ease off."

"He's still a miserable so-and-so," said Tony.

Nigel rounded on him sharply.

"That's enough! He's your company commander and

don't you forget it! And get your hair cut – you're starting to look like one of the girls who serve in the men's canteen!"

A fortnight after we got back from Battle School, a naval commander gave the whole battalion a lecture, with slides, in the camp cinema. He told us that as a result of the landings in North Africa, Sicily and Italy, the Royal Navy had accumulated a great deal of experience and was preparing to mount the largest seaborne landing in its history, of which we would be part.

"Obviously, I don't know where you'll be going, and I wouldn't be allowed to tell you if I did," he said. "However, as far as you are concerned, the drill will be as follows. First, you will board an LSI, which is short for Landing Ship Infantry. Most LSIs are former passenger liners or cross-channel ferries converted to carry LCAs, that is, Landing Craft Assault. You will remain aboard the LSI until you are seven miles from the objective, then transfer to the LCAs, which will be lowered into the sea. Once you are all afloat, the LCAs will line up and head for the beach. The operation will be controlled by someone like me from a motor launch, the advantage being that he has radio contact with the overall commander of that landing sector and knows the situation on the beach ahead.

"If the weather is bad, you won't find the LCAs comfortable – they're almost flat-bottomed and they pitch and roll a lot. As if that isn't bad enough, they are blunt-bowed because of the landing ramp you'll use to get ashore, and a lot of spray comes inboard in any sort of choppy sea. We call them 'kipper boxes' for obvious reasons, but they'll get you there and give you some protection against the enemy's fire as well. Are there any questions so far?"

"What about our supporting armour?" asked Colonel Armitage. "And when can we expect our Support Company's heavy weapons to arrive – the anti-tank guns, mortars and so on?"

"Most of the tanks will come ashore directly from Landing Ships and Landing Craft Tank," replied the Commander. "The idea is that they will touch down some minutes ahead of you. That way you'll find that Jerry's attention will be fully occupied by the time you put in an appearance."

A murmur of approval went round the hall. I was a little puzzled by his use of the word "most" and it would be some months yet before I understood why he had used it.

"As for your own heavy weapons," the Commander continued, "you can expect them to arrive in the follow-up wave. Your transport lorries have a lower priority and will be landed as soon as you've captured sufficient ground ashore."

He went on to describe some of the specialized landing craft that the Navy had produced to accompany our amphibious assault. There were landing craft armed with guns, rockets and bomb-throwers, all designed to deal with some aspect of the enemy's defences. In fact, there seemed to be a landing craft for every conceivable job, including one fitted with stretchers that could ferry casualties out to the waiting hospital ships.

"Nevertheless," continued the Commander, "we're not letting you and the landing craft crews have all the fun. Before you go in, the enemy's defences will have received one almighty battering from our battleships, cruisers and destroyers. As if that isn't enough, bombers from the RAF and US Army Air Force will give them another battering, and you'll have continuous fighter cover all the way. I can promise you this – it's going to be a very noisy party indeed! Anyway, we're going to give you a dry run next month – give you a chance to get some good sea air into your lungs and play about in the sand a bit!"

This produced laughter and a mutter of approval. I think we all looked forward to this exercise as a break in the training routine.

In the middle of November 1943 the battalion made a day-long journey by troop train, reaching Cardiff docks in darkness. I could just make out the name *Countess of Antrim* on the stern of the LSI we were boarding. Everything went like clockwork, for the ship's crew had done this many times, although none of us had been aboard a Royal Navy ship before and it showed immediately. Unfortunately, Three Platoon tried to walk down the steep companionways as though they were stairs. Inevitably, someone's hobnailed boot skidded on a steel tread, and the result was that those below him were swept away by his fall. The tangle of protesting bodies at the foot of the companionway caused the seamen much amusement, as it did to those of us who were not involved. As it sorted itself out I felt a certain amount of guilty pleasure that Grover was at the bottom of the pile. Winded and bruised, he picked himself up, swearing horribly that someone had done it on purpose to spite him.

Shortly after, the ship moved out into the Bristol Channel. I managed to get some rest on one of the bunks in the officers' quarters, but when the steady thump of the ship's engines slowed I knew that we were somewhere off the Welsh Gower Peninsula, where our landing was to take place. A moment later the Tannoy loudspeaker crackled into life, telling us to report to our allocated landing-craft stations. I reached the deck to find a sleet-laden wind blowing. I made my way forward in total darkness to No 4 Port Side, where Sergeant Warriner had just finished calling the roll.

"All present and correct, sir!" he reported.

"Get your troops aboard the landing craft, if you please, gentlemen!" shouted a petty officer.

We clambered over the ship's rail and into the craft. I made my way to where the craft's commander, a young midshipman, was standing beside the small armoured structure in which the coxswain, responsible for steering the craft, stood behind his wheel. When the midshipman was satisfied that everyone was aboard he gave the order to lower away. As we were lowered down the ship's side into the sea, the craft's engine burst into life and we moved away into open water. The men settled themselves in a crowded huddle on the deck. The craft was pitching and rolling in a series of sharp jerks and whenever the blunt bow smashed into a wave, spray flew back at us. This, together, with the sleet, meant that we were soon soaked to the skin. A light blinked to starboard.

"Control launch," explained the midshipman. "Everyone seems to be lined up, so let's go. Full ahead, coxswain, steer oh-one-oh."

"Oh-one-oh it is, sir," replied the coxswain.

The engine note rose to full power as the craft headed for the distant shoreline, still invisible in the darkness. The journey took longer than I had expected and it was obvious that the men, drenched with flying spray from time to time, were not enjoying it. Looking over the side, I could see the bow waves of the other landing craft on either side. It all looked most impressive. At length the sky to the east began to lighten. Ahead lay a low black smudge that I took to be land. The details of this became clearer as the light strengthened into a grey twilight. I knew that this was only an exercise, but it was as close to the real thing as we would get for a while, and it was exciting.

"Touch down in five minutes," said the midshipman. "We'll get you up the beach as far as we can – save you getting your feet wet."

"Stand by," I said as I made my way forward to the ramp through the huddle of packed bodies. Soaked, cold and cramped as they were, the Platoon seemed only too glad that an end to their misery was in sight.

The craft slid smoothly up the sand and the ramp dropped.

"Come on!" I yelled, dashing across it with the Platoon streaming after me. We had been given a full briefing before we left camp and I quickly identified the landmarks that indicated the position of our first objective. We charged across the beach and into the sandhills, where we worked round the flank of the "enemy" position, then attacked it. Knowing that one day we would be doing this in the face of a real enemy, I hoped that it would be as easy. After taking the objective, we moved inland, eliminating pockets of "resistance," then started digging in as C and D Companies passed through to take their own objectives. The "opposition" was provided by a local Home Guard unit who fired blank ammunition and threw thunderflashes at us. They were middle-aged men, most of whom wore Great War medal ribbons. Their commander, a captain about the same age as my father, also wore the ribbon of the Military Cross.

"Bit of a lark, really," he said to me. "Still, it does get you familiar with your landing drills, I suppose."

I had a feeling that he wanted to tell me something, but wasn't quite sure what.

"Have you been involved with an amphibious landing before?" I asked.

"Yes, I was at Gallipoli in 1915," he replied. "Came ashore in unprotected ships' boats, we did. The Turks just fired into the mass of us with their machine guns. So crowded together we were, you never knew whether the man next to you was alive, dead or dying. Still, we got the job done."

I already knew that some of the Gallipoli landings had been a bloodbath and did not know quite what to say. He regarded me with kindly but shrewd eyes and must have seen my concerned expression.

"Now don't you go worrying about that," he continued, patting me on the shoulder. "We've all learned a lot since then. You're better trained and better equipped than we ever were, and you've got proper landing craft, too. All I'm saying is, when the day comes, don't take anything for granted."

At the de-briefing, everyone seemed pleased with the

way the exercise had gone. Even Duncan Flint was in an affable mood and congratulated us. When I complained that according to the exercise umpires my platoon had sustained eighteen casualties as we came ashore, he simply laughed.

"Well, they've got to award you something, haven't they?" he said. "After all, yours was one of the first platoons to cross the beach! Still, it's better than being wiped out, isn't it?"

Once they had dried out, even the troops seemed to have enjoyed themselves. Returning from the de-briefing, I found my platoon sitting round in groups, laughing and joking among themselves.

"Well done, Three Platoon," I said. "The umpires say that some of us were killed, but those who survived did a great job."

"Bit of a doddle, really," said Helsby-Frodsham, when the laughter had died down.

"If the real thing's as easy as that, sir, then let's get on with it, that's what I say," added Corporal Gray.

"Just one thing, sir," chimed in the irrepressible Haggerty. "Them landing craft are a disgrace – can't you get someone to fit 'em with nice comfortable seats?"

I had some reservations about the exercise, partly because of my conversation with the Home Guard captain, so as we route-marched into Swansea, where a train was to take us back to East Anglia, I asked Sergeant Warriner what he thought of it.

"As an exercise, very good, sir," he answered in his flat, matter-of-fact way. "Very good indeed. Can't be faulted."

"But?" I said, knowing that he was holding something back.

"It was an exercise, that's all, sir," he replied, glancing at me sharply.

"And if it had been the real thing?"

"We'll know about the real thing when it happens, sir. Until then, neither of us will be any the wiser."

And with that I had to be content.

I was lucky enough to be sent on leave with half the battalion at Christmas, the other half going at New Year. Turkeys were in short supply, but Mother had managed to find a duck. One day, I thought, there would be better Christmases, but before that happened I would have a war to fight.

In January 1944 we all attended another lecture in the camp cinema. It was given by a senior officer of the Royal Engineers and the subject was Hitler's Atlantic Wall, which was the term used for the German coastal defences stretching from Denmark to the Spanish frontier. Much emphasis was placed on the French coast, which was another indication of where we would be going. Below the high-water mark there were obstacles intended to impale landing craft. These obstacles consisted of wooden stakes or "hedgehogs" made from pieces of angle-iron welded together. Both were fitted with explosive charges. The beaches were mined and, where a sea wall did not exist, concrete walls had been built to prevent tanks leaving them. Then there were the coastal artillery batteries, their huge guns encased in massive steel and concrete bunkers. More bunkers, sited to sweep the beach with their fire, contained anti-tank and machine guns. Behind the beach defences there were anti-tank ditches. These seemed to be covered by fire from concrete pillboxes and trenches nearby, most of which were surrounded by barbed wire and minefields. Every building overlooking the sea had also been turned into a miniature fortress. In addition, we were told that the German field artillery batteries, located some way inland, would add the weight of their fire to the beach defences. The engineer officer could not have given us more to worry about if he had tried, but suddenly the whole tone of his lecture changed.

"Yes, I agree that it looks like a very tough nut to crack," he said. "However, since the Dieppe raid we have produced the means of dealing with every single aspect of these defences. I cannot tell you what they are, but they have been thoroughly tested and they work. Everyone knows that in this sort of operation it will be you, the infantry, who will be most at risk, and everyone is working hard to ensure that your casualties will be kept to an absolute minimum."

After the lecture, Nigel, John, Tony and I discussed what form these mysterious means might take. Sergeant Warriner had told me that, at Alamein, gaps in some of the enemy's minefields had been cleared by flail tanks. These were old Matilda tanks on the front of which was a revolving drum fitted with chains. When it turned the chains flew out and battered the ground, exploding the mines ahead of the tank. We all agreed that similar tanks would probably be used, but had no idea how the other problems were to be dealt with.

The following week we were given our objectives, although we did not know their names or even where they were. After crossing the beach and the sea wall, A Company was to take three houses about 100 yards inland. On our left, B Company had a similar task. We were then to take a hamlet half a mile inland. A mile beyond this, we were to take a large chateau, its outbuilding and nearby cottages, then C and D Companies were to go into the lead. When they had taken their objectives, another of our brigade's battalions was to pass through while we reorganized and consolidated our gains.

Everyone – officers, NCOs and privates alike – studied

the objectives in great detail. We made sand-table models of them and constructed full-scale replicas on the training area. Every so often the RAF would send us their latest batch of air-reconnaissance photographs, some taken from high above and others at low level, and we would incorporate any changes that seemed to have been made in the defences. We also received some pre-war picture postcards of the area, with the names carefully concealed. I got to know the location so well that I could have found my way round it blindfold. We practised attacking the objectives from every direction, with and without tank support, until we had worked out the best possible plan.

During this time we also received more lectures. The first was from another naval officer who told us how the warships lying offshore would continue to give us gunfire support long after we had landed. This would be controlled by a specially trained observer who would accompany us and identify targets by radio. He also showed us some slides to illustrate the devastating effect of naval gunfire on land targets. Next, a Royal Artillery officer described how, once the guns were ashore, it was possible not only to focus the fire of several batteries, or even regiments, on to a target, but also switch it around the battlefield at short notice, as required. Then, an RAF wing commander told us how we would be given close air support. This would involve a forward air controller, an RAF officer who could see the target from a pilot's point of view and relate it to landmarks on the ground. These skills enabled him to "talk in" a strike by ground-attack aircraft. More often than not, he said, they would be rocket-firing Typhoons. Each rocket, he told us, was as powerful as an 8-inch shell. We were all very encouraged by what we had been told.

It was at the end of February 1944 that we learned that Field Marshal Rommel had been appointed commander of the enemy's Army Group B in north-west France. Everyone was aware of Rommel's reputation as a dashing commander during the desert war in North Africa. However, as Sergeant Warriner pointed out, he had been decisively defeated at El Alamein by the very man who was to lead our army when it invaded France, General Montgomery.

In his own way Private Allen, my batman, was also preparing for the invasion. One day he asked me for seven shillings and six pence. When I asked him why, he replied: "I have purchased a small stove and a supply of paraffin tablets from a friend who used to go camping before the War, sir. It occurred to me that in quieter moments we would enjoy a cup of tea. I remember Mr Boris Karloff saying how much he enjoyed my tea. Mr Karloff, you'll remember, sir, played Frankenstein's monster in films. He's English, you know, and Karloff is not his real name, of course. He always said he couldn't get a decent cup of tea in Hollywood, and. . ."

"Well done. Good idea," I said, hurriedly handing over the money. I little thought then that Allen and his little stove would earn a paragraph in the regimental history.

Early in April 1944 we were sent on a week's embarkation leave, which meant that we would soon be going overseas. I can't say that I enjoyed it, because while my parents tried hard to seem cheerful I could see that they were worried, and I simply wanted to get on with whatever lay ahead. Shortly after I returned to camp we received orders to move. The stores were piled on to our own lorries and the troops clambered aboard a convoy of Royal Army Service Corps (RASC) troop transport lorries. Apart from a handful in battalion headquarters, none of us knew where we were bound, and the RASC declined to comment. I could tell from the sun that we were heading steadily west and then south, but as all the signposts had been removed when it was thought the country might be invaded, I had no idea where we were. During the journey we saw many other convoys, American as well as British, consisting of lorried infantry, tanks, Bren carriers, towed guns, self-propelled guns and vehicles from every branch of the army, their progress carefully regulated by the Military Police in their red caps. Sometimes a convoy would join ours for a while, then turn off along a side road, and sometimes we would join someone else's convoy before turning off. I began to marvel at the organizational skill that enabled thousands of vehicles and tens of thousands of men to travel simultaneously towards their given destinations.

It was dusk when we passed through a checkpoint, on either side of which a barbed-wire fence stretched out across the countryside. In the distance I could see armed patrols moving along the fence. I guessed that we were somewhere in the south of England. We travelled on for another 30 minutes before turning off into a large field, surrounded by more barbed wire, in which a tented camp had been set up. Before we dispersed to our tents, we were formed into a hollow square and addressed by Colonel Armitage.

"We are now in the assembly area for the invasion of France," he said. "We are, therefore, considered to be on active service. For security reasons, all of southern England has been sealed off from the rest of the country. No one will be permitted to leave, for any reason whatsoever. The boundary of the secure area is under constant watch by armed patrols and the police. Anyone attempting to breach this cordon will be tried immediately by court martial and I do not have to remind you that desertion in the face of the enemy is a crime for which the death penalty can be imposed. It is no longer possible for you to make telephone calls. You may write letters, although these will be censored in the usual way and will not enter the postal system until we have left. Incoming mail addressed to our old camp in East Anglia will be delivered here.

"We have all trained hard for this moment. We have studied the enemy's defences and decided how they can be overcome. We already know that we can expect maximum support from the Royal Navy and the RAF, but during the next few days we are going to meet some more people who can help us smash a hole right through Hitler's Atlantic Wall."

My feelings on hearing this were mixed. I felt as though a door had closed behind me and that I would not go through it again until the War was over, assuming that I survived. I also felt that I had become a tiny cog in a machine so huge that I could not begin to understand its size.

Next morning I could see that every field stretching to the horizon was occupied by infantry, tank, artillery and engineer units. Overhead, fighter aircraft patrolled ceaselessly, keeping the prying eyes of German aircraft at a safe distance. That afternoon we marched along the road to a copse in which Sherman tanks were parked under camouflage nets. I could see at once that they were nothing like any of the Shermans we had seen before, for they were fitted with two propellers low down at the back and surrounded by a girdle of what looked like folded canvas.

We gathered round a cheerful captain who was standing on the engine deck of one of the tanks.

"Let me introduce us," he said. "We are half of C Squadron, The Flintshire Yeomanry, and we'll be going ashore at the same place you are. In fact, we'll be going ashore just ahead of you to make sure that Jerry's attention is fully occupied by the time you arrive. Our tanks are Sherman DDs, which stands for Duplex Drive, or just DDs for short."

He turned towards the next DD with a shout of, "Right-ho, Sergeant Morris!" There was a hiss of compressed air and the folded canvas suddenly rose into a screen that concealed all of the tank except the tracks. There was a murmur of surprise.

"That is our floatation screen," continued the Captain. "When it's erected, we can float, and the propellers drive us along in the water. As soon as we reach the beach, we collapse the screens, engage the drive and fight like a normal tank."

He paused for a moment.

"The idea is that we are launched from our Landing Ship Tank, or LST, some way out to sea. The tank itself will be under water, suspended from the floatation screen. From the shore, we will simply look like a group of ship's boats – rather smaller, in fact, as there are only a few inches between the top of the screen and the water."

"Doesn't that mean you're in danger of being swamped if there's any sort of rough sea running?" asked Colonel Armitage.

"Yes, Colonel, it has been known," replied the Captain, grinning. "That's why we'll be wearing life jackets. If conditions are too rough, we'll just have to land direct from our LSTs, but we'll still give Jerry an unpleasant surprise."

"Either way, you'll still have to get through the beach obstacles, won't you?"

"True, Colonel, but they will have been dealt with by naval demolition teams – that is, frogmen. They will time their swim to reach the obstacles when they are covered by high tide. They will neutralize Jerry's own charges, then clear gaps in the obstacles for the rest of us to go through. The gaps will be clearly visible at half tide."

The DDs were a revelation to me, but there were more surprises in store. That evening I wandered into a large wood where I found more unfamiliar armoured vehicles, all heavily camouflaged. I was met by a Royal Engineer officer of about my own age who told me that they belonged to the assault squadron that would overcome the fortifications on our sector. He pointed out some flail tanks, which I recognized from Sergeant Warriner's description of those used at El Alamein, although these were based on the Sherman and known as Crabs. He told me that once they had cleared a path through the minefield they would stop flailing and fight as conventional tanks. He then pointed out as strange a collection of vehicles as I have ever seen.

"These are our AVREs," he said proudly. "AVRE stands for Assault Vehicle Royal Engineers."

"What kind of gun is that?" I asked, indicating the stubby barrel protruding from the front of the turret.

"It's a mortar, actually," he replied. "It fires a bomb, called General Wade's Flying Dustbin, to a range of 90 yards. It's designed to crack open the steel and concrete of the enemy's bunkers."

Next, he pointed to two AVREs, one with a large iron-girder bridge attached to its front and the other carrying an enormous bundle of brushwood wrapped round with chains.

"Here's one of our bridgelayers," he said. "We can lay the bridge against a sea wall so that other vehicles can cross it. The AVRE next to it is a fascine carrier. The brushwood bundle, or fascine, can be dropped into an anti-tank ditch and becomes a causeway that other tanks can cross. The AVRE can be used for all sorts of other jobs, too."

I was astonished by these wonderful machines. Their existence, known only to those who manned them and very few others, was one of the best-kept secrets of the War.

The following day all the battalion's officers spent time with those of the DD and assault squadrons. We learned that they too had practised on mock-ups of the enemy defences. We worked out which areas would cause each of us problems and how we could solve these by working together. The commander of the assault squadron told us how his teams would operate. First, the Crabs would flail a path through the minefield to the sea wall, then turn to one side. Then, AVREs would lay their bridges against the sea wall, to create ramps. Next, the fascine AVREs would climb the ramp and drop their brushwood bundles into the anti-tank ditch beyond. The DDs would follow, providing fire support for our attack on the houses and strongpoints. In addition, the assault team possessed armoured bulldozers that could uproot obstacles and fill in craters. When he was asked what would happen if one or more of the vehicles in his assault teams was knocked out he replied that this had been allowed for and sufficient numbers would remain to complete the task.

During the night I heard the DDs and the assault squadron moving off and guessed that they were being embarked aboard their LSTs. Later in the day we were issued with ammunition and rations for the landing, and that afternoon the Support Company's vehicles and anti-tank guns left for the embarkation area. The rifle companies were told they would be leaving next.

As it happened, it was my turn to be orderly officer. I was walking around the camp's perimeter fence at about midnight when I saw movement in the distance. As I ran towards it I saw a figure laying a plank across the barbed wire. Obviously, someone was trying to desert.

"Stop where you are!" I shouted, loosening my revolver in its holster.

The figure turned and I recognized it at once.

"Where d'you think you're going, Grover?" I asked.

He loomed out of the darkness, full of menace.

"Get out of me way!" he snarled. "I told you – I'm not gettin' me head blown off in any bleedin' invasion, not for you or anyone else! So you'll just clear off, sonny, if you know what's good for you! Try and stop me and I'll kill you!"

"No you won't," I replied, drawing my revolver. "For a start, I'm armed and you're not."

He paused warily, but was obviously waiting for me to drop my guard before he pounced.

"Think about what you're doing," I continued. "Once you're over the fence you stand a good chance of being picked up by one of the patrols. If they're American, they might be trigger happy and shoot you on sight. If they're British, you'll face a court martial and a firing squad. But let's suppose you get through, what then? You've no papers, you won't get work or a place to live. You'll spend years on the run and at the end of it you'll still be caught and face a court martial. Is it worth it?"

I could feel his hatred as though it was a physical force.

"Yeah, it's fine for your sort," he said. "Had it made from the moment you were born, didn't you? You make me sick. And what have I got to come back to? Nothing!"

"Let me tell you something," I replied. "Once we're over there, Jerry couldn't care less where we come from or anything else about us. To him, we'll just be targets to be shot at, and as far as that goes we'll all be equal. At least you'll come home with a bit of respect for yourself and that's better than looking in the mirror and seeing a coward."

He swore horribly and looked away. All the aggression seemed to have evaporated. At that moment I was sick of him and everything about him.

"You can desert if you want to, Grover," I said. "I won't stop you. You're no use to me, you're no use to the rest of the Platoon and you're no use to yourself. We'll all be better off without you. Suit yourself."

With the odds stacked so heavily against him, I was reasonably sure that he would stay, but I was taking a calculated risk. If he went, his departure would be welcomed by everyone, but if it ever became known that I had let him go I would be in serious trouble for breaking the disciplinary code. The best I could expect was a severe reprimand from the divisional commander, and the worst a court martial. Against this, if he stayed I would have done my duty and he might just pull himself together.

"Very clever, aren't you, Mister Bleedin' Second Lieutenant Pope?" he said after a moment's indecision, then turned and disappeared among the tents. I was suddenly aware of Sergeant Warriner emerging from the shadows.

"Been expecting this," he said. "Had my eye on him. You handled it well, sir. You can charge him with attempted desertion and gross insubordination if you want to."

"I don't," I replied. "Any other time I'd have thrown the entire book at him. Just now, however, I had the impression that he'd looked himself in the face for the first time and didn't like what he saw. So, either we lose a deadbeat or we get someone who'll pull his weight. Can't lose, can we?"

The Sergeant gave one of his short laughs.

"Ha! Nineteen now, aren't you, sir?"

"Yes, why?" I replied, irritated by the question.

"Nineteen going on thirty – you'll do all right for me, sir!" he said, turning away. "Good night."

I wondered if I *would* be all right when the time came, or whether I would be found wanting. If I made a mistake, the result would not just be another roasting from Duncan Flint, but lost lives. For a moment I felt the heavy burden of responsibility, then realized that there was no escape from it.

3 – 6 June 1944

During the early afternoon of 3 June a convoy of RASC lorries arrived to carry the battalion to Southampton, its port of embarkation. The journey was slow, with frequent halts caused by the volume of traffic heading for the port, so that it was not until evening that we reached the quayside. After a roll call, we marched along the line of moored LSIs. We halted alongside our old friend the *Countess of Antrim* and were directed aboard. Everything seemed pleasantly familiar. Hardly had the last man set foot on deck than the embarkation gangways were removed, the mooring lines were cast off, the engines began to throb and the distance between the ship and the quayside began to widen steadily.

I was startled by the speed at which it happened. I had expected something like a band to play us off or a rousing speech from a general, but instead there was only the bustle of quiet efficiency. However, if I was surprised by the speed of our departure, I was equally surprised when we dropped anchor only a mile or two off the English coast. In the gathering dusk I could see the outline of many other ships anchored nearby, but not their details. A full gale was blowing and there was no incentive to remain on deck. Obviously, it would be impossible for us to make an amphibious landing in those conditions.

After dinner, Duncan Flint distributed maps to his officers. I saw that we would be put ashore at the southern end of the seaside resort of St Grégoire-sur-Mer, that the name of the inland hamlet we were to take was St Grégoire Le Petit and that the château was called Flambard-Chambourcy.

"We're going to Normandy!" exclaimed Nigel, running his finger along the line of coastal resorts. "I've already been to some of these places."

"Normandy?" I said in surprise. "But I thought that we'd use the shortest crossing, and that's from Dover to Calais!"

"That's what Jerry thinks, too," said Duncan Flint. "So we're going in somewhere else!"

I remembered the Major's advice about treating the enemy to a dose of the unexpected.

"Now listen," continued the Major. "I know I've pushed you very hard since I arrived. I expect that there have been times when you've called me a name or two among yourselves."

"Yes, that's right," murmured Tony. The Major ignored him.

"Well, I hope the one thing I've taught you is to think for yourselves. As you'll have gathered, we have been planning this operation for years and every possible contingency has been allowed for. Yet my experience has always been that however carefully an operation is planned some things start to go wrong from the very beginning. If that weren't the case, there would be no need for officers. As it is, we'll have to sort out whatever does go wrong, and quickly too. So, within the context of the battalion and company plans, use your initiative. Now go and brief your platoons."

The gale continued throughout the following day, with the ship pulling hard against her anchor chain. Her officers said that even if we crossed the Channel they would not be able to get us ashore, so we would have to make the best of it until the weather improved. On 5 June the weather began to moderate, but was still very unpleasant. The troops, who had been keyed up for the assault, began to grumble at being confined below decks. Then, at about 14:00, the anchor came clattering up, the engines began their steady thumping and we headed slowly out to sea. By late evening we had reached a point in mid-Channel and slowed to a standstill, surrounded by hundreds more ships of every type, including more LSIs, LSTs and many types I could not identify. Destroyers fussed around the lines like sheep dogs, shepherding vessels into the correct order. I spotted the midshipman who had commanded our landing craft during our exercise off the Gower Peninsula.

"Does this mean we're going in, then?" I asked.

"Looks that way," he replied. "The forecast for tomorrow promises some improvement, but there'll still be a nasty sea running. Still, Jerry won't be expecting us in this sort of weather, and that's a bonus."

"Won't he have lain minefields off the French coast?"

"Oh, yes, but they'll be some way out. Anyway, our minesweepers will be clearing lanes through them, if they haven't done so already."

Shortly after, we received official confirmation that we would land at 07:35 next morning, which meant that we would start boarding the landing craft at 05:00. Now that we knew what was happening, everyone's spirits rose. "Good. Let's get on with it – we're fed up waiting around out here," was the Platoon's general view when I passed on the news.

Towards dusk, the whole mass of shipping began moving slowly southwards in the direction of Normandy.

I had grown used to the almost permanent presence of our fighter aircraft during daylight hours, and to the drone of heavy bombers at night. On the night of 5 June, however, that drone was multiplied many times over. I did not know it then, but one British and two American airborne divisions were about to parachute on to what would become the northern and southern flanks of the beachhead.

At about 04:30 Sergeant Warriner and I inspected the

Platoon's equipment, arms, ammunition and rations. A cheerful sailor came round, handing out cans from a box.

"Self-heating soup, mate," he explained. "You'll have a long cold run in and you'll be glad of it. Instructions are on the can. You'll be pleased to hear that the RAF has started beating the daylights out of Jerry."

I had been conscious of the constant roar of aircraft engines for over an hour. Even so, everyone was feeling on edge, so it was a relief when we were ordered to our landing craft stations. Because of an overcast sky it was still dark when we reached the deck. The French coast was invisible, but I could see the flash of explosions and the glow of fires in that direction. As I clambered aboard the landing craft I saw that three lightweight ladders had been stowed along one side of the craft, as we had been promised. These were intended to help us cross the sea wall and the section commanders had already detailed the men who were to carry them.

We were lowered into the sea without incident, but not even the exercise off the Gower had prepared me for the sea's ugly movement when we left the ship's side. The gale had certainly abated, but there was a huge swell moving crossways beneath us, so severe that in addition to the motion I'd expected (and the clouds of flying spray), the craft seemed to slide sideways down those heaving mounds of water. As the light became stronger I could see more of our landing craft forming up into an assault wave. The sea was covered with ships as far as the eye could see, many of them flying large silver balloons trailing thick wires to deter low-level air attacks. Overhead, I could hear more bombers heading for the coast to continue their remorseless battering of the enemy's defences. Then came the squadrons of fighters, ready to pounce on any intervention by German aircraft, though none appeared.

After a while, I was conscious that we should have commenced our run in towards the coast. However, we remained more or less stationary, although the midshipman occasionally manoeuvred the craft to allow for the tide having carried us away from our correct position. I had hoped to reach the beach with a fit, aggressive platoon, and the longer we remained afloat the less likely this became. In fact, some of the men had already begun to vomit and many of the rest were looking green and sweaty.

"What's happening?" I asked the midshipman at length.

"I don't know," he replied. "Some sort of hold-up ahead. Maybe the LSTs have had trouble getting in."

As I watched the last of the bombers making their way back to England, there was a sudden distant flash far away to our left. I could see a battleship, wreathed in smoke, and seconds later the roar of her guns reached us. Then, every warship in sight seemed to open fire – battleships, monitors and cruisers, all filling the air with furious sound and blasting the enemy's defences with tons of high explosive every minute. I knew I was watching history being made, but at that precise moment I felt too sick to care.

"Here we go," said the midshipman in response to some unseen signal. The engine note rose to full power as we pushed steadily ahead. I glanced over my shoulder at the fast-receding *Countess of Antrim*, conscious that we were leaving our last link with home.

The craft's motion eased somewhat now that we were moving. I began to feel better and took more interest in what was going on. The lines of landing craft forging ahead were themselves an impressive sight. As the coast came into view I could see explosions and fires raging ashore. We passed through destroyers pounding away as hard as they could. Shells began to burst round us, sending splinters clattering off the hull. Minutes later we passed a craft of some sort, on fire and sinking, with men floundering in the water. I was horrified, but there could be no question of our stopping to pick them up without becoming a target ourselves, and in any event people were depending on us to do our own job.

"It's not all one-sided, is it?" I said.

"Never is," replied the midshipman levelly.

The incident made me realize that we were only minutes away from sustaining casualties of our own. During the months we had been together, I had grown to like the men of Three Platoon, and now it was inevitable that some of us would not live to see the end of the day. I looked round their stolid, friendly faces. Some were seasick, but all were impassive, keeping their fear locked away from the others. I knew that I was doing likewise, because my own fear had begun to grip me in its icy hand.

We passed a Landing Craft Rocket just as it sent salvo after salvo of its missiles streaking whoosh-whoosh-whoosh towards the beach minefields. Now I could see the three houses we were to take, instantly recognizable from our constant study of air photographs. I could also see the lines of semi-submerged stakes and iron hedgehogs and, beyond them, lines of LSTs crowded together at the water's edge. Nearby, a Landing Craft Gun was banging away at the beach defences. On our own craft a seaman was manning a machine gun, rattling away at an unseen target. The combined level of noise was such that we barely heard the enemy's rounds striking the ramp. The seaman slumped behind the gun mounting with a dark stain of blood spreading across his left shoulder.

"Starboard ten!" said the midshipman sharply, then "Midships!"

I could see a light flashing from the control motor launch and that the battalion's landing craft had all turned on to this new heading. With growing alarm I pointed out that this was taking us away from our objective. The

84

midshipman explained that because of the congestion he couldn't get us in where we should be, but would drop us as close as he could.

"Port ten – take her in!" he said a moment later, then turned to me, a smile creasing his normally dour expression.

"Away you go – give 'em hell!" he said as we shook hands.

As I made my way forward I suddenly remembered the Home Guard captain's description of Gallipoli and wondered whether the landing craft's interior would be swept by machine-gun fire when the ramp went down, turning it into a shambles of dead and dying. Chilling fear fought with the residue of seasickness in my stomach. My legs felt so leaden that it was an effort of will to get them to move.

"We've come in too far to the right!" I heard myself shouting to the Platoon. "Bear left as soon as we're ashore and run like hell! The sooner we get under the cover of the sea wall the better!"

The men, their faces set, nodded dumbly. There was a screech of tortured metal as we scraped past one of the obstacles, an iron framework known as Element C. I was horrified to see that a large explosive charge was attached to it. To my intense relief, the charge did not detonate, but I had no time to reflect on the subject as the craft slithered to a standstill on the sand and the ramp went down.

"Come on!" I yelled as I ran down it, then slopped through a few yards of water to reach dry land. As I pounded over the beach I could see the entire shoreline. The rest of the company, and B Company beyond, were all running hard for the sea wall. Here and there a man dropped. Others were being helped to safety by their comrades. In the distance a DD was burning, but more DDs were pumping shells into the fire slits of the concrete beach bunkers. A bridge AVRE leaned at an angle, its track shot off. Crabs were flailing paths up to the sea wall and more vehicles were pouring out of the LSTs. Green tracer from an enemy machine-gun post began to flash past me from left to right, about thirty yards ahead. I thought I would die when I reached it, but kept running. It stopped, possibly because one of the DDs had neutralized the post. Mortar bombs began to explode nearby. Behind me I could hear Sergeant Warriner's bellow as he urged the men on:

"C'MON, MOVE YOURSELVES! MOVE! MOVE! MOVE! D'YOU THINK WE'VE BROUGHT YOU TO THE SEASIDE SO YOU COULD MUCK AROUND IN THE SAND?"

I found the going hard, and for those who were worse affected by seasickness it must have been torture. I reached the sea wall panting and estimated that I had run approximately 350 yards. To my left a Crab had finished flailing its lane and was moving to one side as a bridge

AVRE approached. The wall itself was covered in barbed wire and would have been impossible to climb without the ladders. Gasping, the Platoon arrived. In their wake I could see two or three of them sprawled on the sand, and two more helping a third towards the wall.

I ran up the first of the ladders to be placed and jumped over the promenade railings. The whole area beyond was pitted with craters from the naval bombardment.

"Head for the anti-tank ditch!" I shouted as more of the men joined me. "Use the craters for cover and move in short rushes."

We were still too far to the right of the three houses, from which the flashes of machine-gun fire had commenced as soon as we appeared. I was shocked to see Corporal Gray flung backwards by a burst just as he reached the top of the ladder. Then we were alternately running and crawling towards the anti-tank ditch, into which we dropped to recover our breath.

"The Major's calling, sir," said Private Helsby-Frodsham, my signaller.

I took the headset from him but all I could hear was mush, broken now and then by an unintelligible word in Duncan Flint's voice.

"Unreadable, out," I said, returning the headset. "What's wrong with this thing? It was working perfectly when we left the ship."

"I got drenched a couple of times in the landing craft," replied Helsby-Frodsham. "There must be salt water in the connectors – I'll dry them off as soon as I get a chance, sir."

Things began to happen very quickly indeed. An AVRE carrying a huge fascine clambered over the ramp placed by the bridgelayer and began crawling towards the anti-tank ditch. From low down in the right-hand house there was a flash and a blast cloud of dust.

"Anti-tank gun in the cellar!" shouted Sergeant Warriner. "Look – you can just see the concrete reinforcement above the window!"

The German gunner could never have seen anything like the AVRE and its fascine in his life, and his shot passed harmlessly through the fascine itself. Getting the fascine into the ditch was critical if the DDs were to support our attack on the houses, so I ran along the ditch, telling each section to concentrate its fire on the anti-tank gun's fire slit. The AVRE continued to waddle forward, halted with a jerk, and the fascine tumbled neatly into the ditch. Our fire must have been having some effect as the anti-tank gun's second shot was off-line and simply grazed the side of the AVRE's turret. The AVRE crossed its fascine, trundled forward for a few yards, then fired its mortar. I could see the bomb for most of its flight and realized why it was called a flying dustbin. The tremendous explosion caused the front of the building to collapse like a house of cards. I saw two machine-gunners who had been firing from an upper window go down with it to be buried under a mound of brickwork and beams that also covered the anti-tank gun's fire slit. My men cheered lustily.

Two DDs were now over the wall. They opened fire on the two remaining houses, eliminating one source of enemy fire after another. I now had to do some quick thinking. The three houses were to have been taken by the company in a frontal attack, but my own platoon's objective had already been eliminated by the AVRE and anyway we were too far to the right to take part in the attack on the other two houses. I decided to swing round the now burning ruin and cut off any of the defenders who tried to escape.

"Right flanking – come on!" I shouted. As we sprinted across the open space I was conscious of the two DDs crossing the fascine and the rest of the company rising from the ditch, bayonets fixed. Once past the houses we swung to the left and, sure enough, about twenty men in field-grey uniforms and coal-scuttle helmets were running from the rear doors.

"Put a long burst into the ground ahead of them!" I shouted to the nearest Bren gunner.

This, together with the levelled bayonets of the Platoon charging towards them, convinced the enemy that they should drop their weapons. They were a sorry lot, most of whom were covered in brick and plaster dust. Many had obviously been shaken by their ordeal, including their officer, who seemed anxious to retain some of his dignity.

"We will counter-attack and throw you back into the sea!" he shouted hysterically in English.

"Shut yer gob or I'll throw you into the sea, mate!" said Haggerty, stripping the man of his Luger pistol and handing it to me.

The rest of the company appeared, grinning. The prisoners were pushed into line and marched off to the beach by two slightly wounded men.

"What's the matter with your radio?" snapped Duncan Flint.

I told him.

"Then how come you carried out my order?" he asked belligerently.

"I didn't receive your order," I replied, irritated. "It seemed like the right thing to do."

"It was. You used your head. Well done. Now let's get on – we're falling behind our timetable."

We began to move inland, accompanied by the two DDs. It did not take us long to reach the hamlet of St Grégoire Le Petit, which had been badly knocked about by the bombardment. We approached it warily, expecting more fighting, but instead the civilian population came out, waving French flags and cheering.

"*Ah, les braves Anglais!*" they shouted. They told us that the Germans had gone, offered us wine and cheese and hugged us. With difficulty we extricated ourselves and continued towards our next objective, the château of Flambard-Chambourcy, passing the wreckage of a German artillery battery, strewn with bodies, on the way. In my ignorance of war I actually began to enjoy myself for a while.

This ended abruptly as we topped a rise. Some 500 yards down the slope lay the château, a large country house flanked by lower wings on either side, with a stable block at the rear. Nearby were the estate's home farm and the cottages of the workers. Extensive woodland stretched across the hillside beyond. No sooner had we appeared than the entire position seemed to sparkle with machine-gun fire coming from every window and many places in the grounds. It was apparent that any attempt to advance further would be suicidal. Instinctively, the Platoon ran for the cover provided by a hedge and ditch just ahead of us. Looking round, I saw that three of my men were down. Almost immediately, mortar rounds began to explode around us. The two DDs arrived, halted and opened fire on the building. After a few rounds one gave a convulsive lurch as it was penetrated by return fire. It began to belch smoke. Four of the five-man crew tumbled out, not a second too soon, for as the last of them hit the ground the tank burst into flames that roared from the hatches like a blowtorch. The second tank reversed back from the crest until only its turret was showing and continued to engage the enemy, changing its position from time to time.

Using my binoculars, I began to examine the German position in detail through the lower branches of the hedge. As well as machine guns and mortars, the enemy had three tracked vehicles in the position. They each seemed to be armed with a powerful anti-tank gun protected by armour plate. I remembered what they were from our recognition lectures on enemy equipment.

"B Company are pinned down on the left, too," said Duncan Flint's voice at my elbow. "Spot anything?"

"Yes," I replied. "The Jerries haven't dug in, so all this must be a bit of a surprise to them. They seem to have three tracked tank-destroyers – one by the summer house, one in the entrance to the stable yard and one by the manure heap in the farmyard."

"Too tough a nut for us to crack on our own," he said after surveying the position himself. His tone was almost friendly. "Just the sort of place Jerry would use to rally troops retreating from the coast as well as feeding in reinforcements from elsewhere, don't you think? A kind of 'hold at all costs' job while he pulls himself together."

Colonel Armitage arrived. After taking in the situation he told us that C and D Companies were coming up and that he would push them round both flanks to take the château from behind. During a pause in the firing I went back to our casualties. One was dead, but with the assistance of Baker, who had been promoted to Lance Corporal shortly before we left East Anglia, I managed to bring in the other two. One's arm was shattered and the other had serious chest wounds. While we bandaged them with field dressings, the other two companies started their attack. They made progress for a while, but were then halted by determined resistance in the woods.

At this point the brigade commander arrived, bringing with him a lieutenant commander who wore his naval insignia on a khaki battledress and was accompanied by a naval signaller. I began to feel that my part of the front was becoming seriously congested with senior officers.

"What the devil is going on here?" snapped the Brigadier testily to Colonel Armitage. "You should be two miles further on! The divisional commander wants results and he wants them now!"

While the Colonel explained the position, I couldn't help chuckling to myself. Everyone in the Army, it seemed, had someone hounding him. I hounded the Platoon, Duncan Flint hounded me, the Colonel hounded Duncan Flint, the Brigadier hounded the Colonel, the Divisional Commander hounded the Brigadier, and so on, right up the chain of command.

"This is one for you, I think, Toby," said the Brigadier, turning to the Naval Gunfire Support Officer (NGSO).

"Just my sort of party," replied the Lieutenant Commander. He settled himself down beside me with his signaller and transmitted the map co-ordinates of the château and the farm.

"We've got HMS *Norseman*," he explained. "She's a cruiser with eight 8-inch guns. Ever seen an 8-inch shell explode?"

I shook my head.

"Then you're in for a treat. First one should be arriving in about 35 seconds." He obviously took enormous pleasure in his work.

There was a sound like ripping cloth as the shell passed overhead. Then a huge fountain of earth, flame and smoke erupted some distance in front of the château.

"Short. Add four hundred," commented the NGSO into his microphone.

The next round exploded beyond the château.

"Down two hundred."

"How many salvos will you give us?" asked Duncan Flint. I could see that a plan was forming in his mind. "And how long between salvos?"

"Five should do the job," replied the Lieutenant Commander. "Assuming that they're nippy aboard, say between 30 and 45 seconds between each. Why?"

"I think that after the second salvo the Jerries will be so stunned and blinded by smoke and dust that we should attack. If you give us six salvos we should be in among 'em before they can recover their wits – those of them that are still alive, that is."

"Good idea, Duncan," said Colonel Armitage. "I'll warn B Company. They can take the farm while you deal with the château."

"Six rounds gunfire, commence, commence, commence!" said the NGSO into his microphone.

The first salvo passed overhead with a gigantic tearing sound. Huge explosions erupted around and among the enemy-held buildings. I saw walls tumbling and roofs collapse. Before the dust had settled the second salvo landed. The whole area was obscured by smoke and flying debris.

"Come, my lucky lads!" shouted Duncan Flint. The company set off at a brisk walk down the long slope. To my relief, there was little or no response from the enemy. I began to count the salvos mentally. After the third the buildings vanished beneath the spreading pall of smoke and dust. As the fourth came in something began to burn, adding thick smoke to the fog. By the time the fifth landed we had quickened our pace to a trot and were approaching the bottom of the slope. The sixth erupted as we reached the balustrade fronting the château's ornamental gardens.

"Charge!" I yelled, vaulting the balustrade. Yelling like fiends we tore across the garden. Great holes had appeared in the walls and roof of the house, through which broken beams and sagging floors were visible.

Somewhere, a fire was raging. Field-grey bodies lay half-buried in rubble. With shouts of *Kamerad!* (*Friend!*) more Germans staggered out of the wreckage, their hands up. They seemed completely dazed, with all the fight knocked out of them.

My responsibility was to clear the wing of the house on the right. We went through the usual house-clearing drill, but met no resistance. The tank destroyer in the entrance to the stable yard had taken a direct hit and been reduced to a tangle of torn metal. As I entered the yard itself, however, a burst of sub-machine gun bullets cracked into the brickwork near my head. I caught sight of a figure in an upper window of the stable block. It dodged out of sight. Mindful of what the AVRE had done to the defenders of the house near the beach, I decided to bring the PIAT gunner forward. While several men kept the window under fire, I directed him to aim his bomb into the wall beside it. The whole room seemed to explode. We charged across the yard and into the stable. One of the Bren gunners fired bursts through the ceiling into the rooms. There was a scream and the sound of a body falling. Blood began to seep through the plaster above. I heard boots running towards the head of the stairs.

"Don't shoot – we surrender!" shouted a voice in German.

"Hold your fire!" I said.

Three frightened German soldiers clattered down the stairs, their hands raised. They were almost incoherent with fear, and I gathered that their sergeant had refused to let them surrender earlier. Now he was dead, and so was one of their comrades. They also told me that the chateau had been used as a regimental headquarters. I ordered them to be frisked and put with the other prisoners. Of the two remaining tank destroyers, one had been knocked out in the farmyard by the DD and the other, having made a run for it, had overturned into a ditch bordering the narrow lane behind the château. There was no sign of the crew.

I may not have liked Duncan Flint, but I had to admit to myself that he was a first-class soldier, as the company had sustained virtually no casualties in the attack. Colonel Armitage said that the resistance experienced by C and D Companies in the woods had melted away as soon as the château fell and that we were to follow on as soon as we had reorganized.

Duncan held a quick orders group. I had not seen John since the previous evening and felt a chill of apprehension when Sergeant Brumby, his platoon sergeant, turned up in his stead.

"Where's Mr Crane?" I asked.

"I should think he's probably on his way back to England

by now, sir," replied the Sergeant. "Stepped on a stray mine while we were running for the sea wall. He'll lose one leg for sure, and the other's a mess."

I couldn't look at Tony Walters, who had always joked that because John commanded One Platoon he would be our first casualty.

"I wish I'd kept my mouth shut," I heard him mutter.

"I dare say you do," snapped Duncan Flint harshly. "In future, just keep your idiotic forecasts to yourself and remember that what happened to John was rotten bad luck, nothing more. Now let's get on."

We followed up C and D Companies and dug in around the crossroads that had been their final objective. As we did so, the brigade's reserve battalion, accompanied by Sherman tanks, passed through us to continue the advance.

"Where've you been?" shouted Haggerty. "Did you get lost?"

"What are you doing, sitting round here?" they yelled back. "You should be halfway to Paris by now!"

Shortly after, the sounds of battle told us that they were in action. I had lost all track of time and was astonished when my watch revealed that it was still early afternoon. A lifetime seemed to have passed since we left the *Countess of Antrim* and England seemed another world away. Our anti-tank guns and mortars arrived. Peter Gresley, the anti-tank platoon commander, told me that the landing beaches looked like a disturbed anthill with men and vehicles travelling in every direction, yet everyone seemed to know what they were doing and where they were going. At about 16:00 the concentrated booming of tank guns could be heard some miles to our left. It rose to a crescendo, fell, rose again and finally ceased. Later, we were told that the enemy's 21st Panzer Division had twice attempted to drive through the beach-head to the sea, but had been beaten off. Suddenly aware that I was ravenously hungry, I gulped down my can of self-heating soup, having forgotten about it until that moment.

Shortly before dusk, the first of the battalion's jeeps and transport vehicles appeared, enabling us to replenish our ammunition. We stood to in our slit trenches for an hour, but nothing happened. Sergeant Warriner had already given me our casualty return – three dead, including Corporal Gray, four seriously wounded who required evacuation, and five slightly wounded: a total of twelve.

"We've got away with it very lightly indeed, believe me, sir," he concluded.

"Yes," I replied, unable to grasp what he had said for a moment. "That's a third less than they gave us during the Gower Peninsula exercise."

Then the full impact struck me. That had been a statistic and this was reality. The slightly wounded would probably come back to us, but the dead had gone for ever and it was unlikely that we would see the seriously wounded again.

I took a turn on guard, then settled into my slit trench. I had seen history made, but just then it seemed less important than the hour or two's sleep that lay ahead.

7 June – 16 August 1944

I cannot remember the details of everything that happened in the weeks after D-Day, for the simple reason that they are all jumbled together in my memory and, for most of the time, I was too exhausted to absorb the sequence in which events took place. I remember hearing that the Americans had sustained heavy casualties getting ashore on one of their landing beaches, and that all our beachheads were now linked together so that we had a continuous front facing the enemy.

I learned, too, yet more secrets about D-Day. After the Dieppe raid, the planners had recognized that we would not be able to capture a French port in working order when we invaded, so under the codename Mulberry we had brought two prefabricated harbours with us. These consisted of large, hollow iron and concrete structures together with lines of old ships that were towed into position and sunk to form breakwaters and protect the harbours from gales. Each harbour contained three floating piers, connected to the shore by floating roadways. Every tug in the country, and more from the United States, had been required to tow these across the Channel. Then there was PLUTO, standing for Pipe Line Under The Ocean, which was an undersea pipeline laid from England to Normandy, that kept us supplied with fuel.

By landing in Normandy, we had certainly taken the Germans by surprise, but there was a price to pay. To the south-west of Caen was a large area of countryside that the French call *bocage*. It consisted of small fields, narrow lanes and high hedgerows growing from earth banks. It was ideal defensive country that enabled the enemy to conceal himself until the last possible moment before opening fire. It also stopped our tanks from giving us their full support, for as soon as they attempted to climb a bank an anti-tank gun would put a round through its exposed belly plates. It therefore became an infantryman's war in which we fought from hedgerow to hedgerow, just as my father's generation had fought from trench to trench in the Great War. We suffered serious casualties, but the enemy, lacking air power and exposed to our terrible naval gunfire and artillery, suffered far more. We now know that Hitler had insanely forbidden them to yield a single yard of ground and we grew to respect their discipline and fortitude. For our part, deadly tiredness was our constant companion. There was little sleep to be had in the short summer nights, for we stood to for an hour after dusk and again for an hour before dawn, and in between we would take our turn on guard.

Even when we were resting out of the line we were still within range of the enemy's heavy guns, which would sometimes send over a shell or two to remind us that they were still there. Much of my time was spent writing letters to my parents or to the next of kin of men who had been killed. The fine sunlit days were mocked by the devastation caused to this pretty countryside. Farms stood ruined and the bloated bodies of cattle caught in the crossfire lay stinking horribly in the fields. Sometimes, Helsby-Frodsham would go foraging in his amiable way and return with cheese and bottles of wine that would be shared among the Platoon.

It was in the *bocage* that Three Platoon won its first decoration. One day at the end of June 1944 we were advancing up a slope towards a hedge when two machine guns opened up, one from each corner of the field, so that their fire overlapped. We dived for cover at once. The slope was concave and, to my relief, the machine guns' fire could not do us much harm as long as we remained pressed to the ground.

Haggerty was lying some yards in front of me, to the right. I saw his pack twitch several times as it was hit. A stain began to spread over his battledress and I feared the worst. Then, he was up and running at the nearest machine gun, a look of berserk fury on his face. His feet seemed to be swept from under him by an unseen hand. As the German shifted his fire to another target, he scrambled up and sprinted the last 20 yards to the gun, which was dug into the earth bank below the hedge. Throwing himself to one side of the fire slit, he posted a grenade through it. Its explosion was followed by screams and the gun fell silent. Meanwhile, the Platoon's Brens, as well as those of Two Platoon, had suppressed the fire of the second machine gun.

"Come on!" I shouted. "Don't leave it all to Haggerty!"

As we charged up the slope I saw Haggerty toss a second grenade into a rifle pit, then fire from the hip into another with his rifle. Caught between him and the advancing company, the surviving Germans emerged with their hands raised in surrender.

"Are you hit?" I said to the panting Haggerty as we began turning round the captured trenches.

"They shot the piggin' heel off me boot, sir," he replied, examining his damaged footwear. There was a strong smell of whisky about him. Duncan Flint arrived, having witnessed the whole incident.

"More to the point, are you drunk?" he asked.

"No, sir!" replied Haggerty indignantly. "Just take a look at this."

He opened his pack to reveal the shattered remains of two whisky bottles. Printed on the soggy labels were the words GOVERNMENT STORES – NOT FOR SALE.

"And how did you come by these?" asked Duncan Flint suspiciously.

"Did a bloke in the Service Corps a favour once, sir," said Haggerty, grinning. "He dropped them by one night when we were out of the line. I was going to share them with the lads. That's why I got mad when Jerry smashed 'em."

We all thought that the truth might be a little different, but despite this he received the Military Medal on Duncan Flint's recommendation.

Once we had fought our way out of the *bocage*, progress should have been easier, but by then the enemy had rushed reinforcements to the front and was resisting fiercely. On one occasion we were holding one side of a hill and the Germans the other. They did everything in their power to stop us taking the crest, which overlooked their positions for miles around. Once they tried a night attack in an attempt to dislodge us. It was led by Tiger tanks, followed by infantry. Our defensive artillery barrage stopped the infantry, but the Tigers came on and began wandering about the battalion's positions. By then, we all knew that tanks were all but blind in the dark and that without their infantry they were almost useless, so we simply lay in our narrow slit trenches, which were invisible to tank commanders within their closed hatches. Allen, oblivious to what was going on, had just brewed tea. A Tiger halted beside our trench, its weight causing the wall to crumble. To his intense annoyance, some of the soil dropped into Allen's steaming mug.

"Really! Some people have no manners at all!" he said. "I'm going to give that man a piece of my mind!"

Before I could stop him, he had clambered out of the trench and aboard the Tiger. Obviously, in the dark he had mistaken the tank for one of the Churchills with which we had worked so often. At that moment the enemy commander opened his hatch in an attempt to get his bearings.

"You really should have more consideration for other people!" shouted Allen before he realized who he was addressing. The two stared incredulously at each other for a second, then Allen flung the scalding contents of his mug into the German's face. With a yell of rage and pain the commander drew his pistol and began blazing wildly into the darkness, but by then Allen had leapt back into the trench. The Tiger moved off with a lurch, only to fall victim to a PIAT bomb fired into its thin stern plate before it had covered 100 yards.

"He was a German, sir – a German!" said Allen in a shocked voice when he had recovered from the surprise. I'm afraid I was too helpless with laughter to offer him any sympathy, as was the rest of the company when the news of his exploit spread. Private Allen was to become a legend as the only man in the regiment to have attacked a Tiger with a mug of hot tea.

There was, in fact, very little to laugh at on that hill. On the morning after the Tiger attack we had just finished the dawn stand-to when I glanced in the direction of Two Platoon. I saw Tony stand up and stretch in his slit trench. He gave me a cheery wave. Then came the rising scream of an incoming heavy calibre shell. The explosion obliterated the trench and no identifiable trace of Tony was ever found. I was deeply saddened and very shaken by the incident, for Tony had been a good friend and now I was the last of A Company's original platoon commanders. I was left with a horrible feeling that it would be my turn next.

"Doesn't work like that, sir," said Sergeant Warriner in his flat matter-of-fact voice. "His number was on that one – yours wasn't, so best leave it at that."

Sometimes Warriner's casual acceptance of death annoyed me, but he was right, of course. Death was our constant companion and our concern had always to be for the living.

We had a short rest period after we were relieved on the hill, then returned to another part of the line. At various times throughout the campaign we received replacements for our casualties, including two officers almost straight from OCTU. Neither of them lasted more than a few days.

One took a sniper's bullet through the head when he stood up to read his map. The other lost his way while leading a night patrol and was listed as missing. The trouble with the replacements generally was that they were neither as thoroughly trained nor as experienced as we were. They were lonely, lost souls and although I did my best to make them feel at home they were not accepted by the rest of the Platoon until they had proved themselves in a couple of actions. One of them, a man called Phillips, was indirectly responsible for the most unlikely of recipients winning our second decoration.

When we returned to the line we took part in a brigade attack. The battalion on our right was unable to capture some high ground, and we were therefore unable to make progress because we were overlooked and under fire from two directions. Duncan Flint ordered us back to our trenches, covered by a smokescreen laid by our 2-inch mortars. Despite this, the enemy continued to rake the area with mortar and machine-gun fire. As the smoke cleared I looked back and saw three members of the Platoon lying in no man's land. Two were not moving but the third, Phillips, was writhing in agony from the wounds he had received. For the moment I estimated that it would be suicidal for anyone to go out and get him. I shouted that he should remain still to avoid losing more blood and that we would bring him in when things quietened down a little. Either he did not hear me or was too frightened to understand, for he continued to try and get up, only to collapse in a heap.

Suddenly a figure ran from our lines towards him. It was Grover. Machine-gun bullets were kicking up the earth round him and mortar rounds were exploding constantly nearby. I could not see how he could possibly survive, but he did. He reached Phillips, heaved him on to his shoulders in a fireman's lift, and ran back.

"What made you do it?" I asked him later.

"'E was like me – no mates," he said, a look of defiance in his eyes. "Could 'ave been me out there and you lot couldn't 'ave cared less. Just thought I'd show the piggin' lot of you."

"That's not true and you know it," I replied.

After that, however, the Platoon's attitude towards Grover changed. Ever since D-Day he had been an unremarkable soldier and I suspected that he had hung back during one or two attacks. Now, however, the men began to regard him with something like respect and shared their jokes and other things with him. As a result of this, he seemed to mellow and began to pull his full weight.

"If your parents had been alive they would have been proud of you," I told him on the day we learned that he had been awarded the Military Medal. "One day you'll have a family of your own. They will be proud, too, because it isn't every kid whose dad has won the MM."

"Yeah, mebbe," he said thoughtfully, as though he had just seen a future for himself. "That would be a turn up."

He looked at me suspiciously, as though I had the power to spoil it for him.

"I said a few things to you before we left England, sir," he said at length. "I was wrong, an' I admit it. What worries me is that you always cracked down on me before, but you didn't for that. Why?"

"I don't remember any such discussion, Grover," I lied. "Whatever it is you're thinking of is best forgotten."

He gave a huge sigh of relief. What passed for a smile crossed his harsh features.

"Thanks, Mr Pope, sir," he said. "I'll not let you down."

A week or two later we had advanced another mile or so and our front lay along a narrow stream in a shallow valley. I was told to report to Duncan Flint, who had set up his company headquarters in the cellar of a cottage.

"Take a look at this," he said, handing me an air-reconnaissance photograph. It showed the long gentle upward slope on the enemy side of the stream, leading to the woodland at the crest, which we knew was the enemy's front line. At first I couldn't see anything remarkable.

"As you know," he continued, "there are several hummocks about 500 yards up the slope. Look closely at this one, under the tree. There are signs of digging.

Could mean Jerry has a standing patrol or an observation post there. The brigadier wants us to take a look tonight – better still, go and get a prisoner! I suggest you move out at 23:45. Right, Andy, off you go – and don't mess up!"

I spent the rest of the day examining the route I would take. I decided to leave Sergeant Warriner in command of the Platoon and take Corporal Baker, Haggerty, Grover and six other men whom I knew I could rely on. During the evening stand-to we blackened our hands and faces, changed from boots into gym shoes and pulled on woollen cap comforters. In addition to our usual weapons we carried trench knives and coshes made from soil-filled socks that would stun rather than kill.

At 23:45 we moved quietly across the shallow stream. Patrolling can be a terrifying experience, because you are literally moving through darkness into unknown territory where the slightest mistake can cost lives. Clouds were passing across the moon and I had decided to take advantage of the shadow cast by a hedge that climbed the slope. Both sides were sending up flares as a matter of routine. When these burst above us we stood stock still, for even in semi-darkness any movement draws the eye. Consequently, our progress was very slow. I led the way, gently swinging a thin stick ahead of me. It touched something. Bending down, I felt a wire stretching in both directions. It was either connected to a flare or a grenade that would have exploded when someone tripped over it. I suppose that the route I had chosen was an obvious one and the enemy was bound to have placed such booby traps along it. By following the wire we located the stake to which it was attached, enabling us to disarm the device. We encountered three more trip wires before we were level with the suspected enemy post. We then crawled across the slope for about 100 yards to avoid being seen by those on the crest. I found myself on the edge of a trench that became deeper and finally entered the back of the hummock.

Just then, Corporal Baker touched me lightly on the shoulder and pointed towards the crest. The trick when trying to identify something in the dark is to look just above it. I saw a figure carrying something walking down the slope towards us. I signalled the patrol to spread out, which they did silently. Then I positioned myself near the start of the trench and stood up.

"*Halt! Wer da?* (Halt! Who's there?)," I hissed, in my best German.

"*Bauer – mit abendessen* (Bauer – with supper)," came the answer.

"*Ach das, gut! Geben Sie es mir.* (Ah, that's good! Give it to me.)"

Obediently, Bauer handed me a box. In an instant he was surrounded and Grover had a knife across his throat. His eyes rolled in terror.

"Keep him quiet," I whispered, then turned to Baker. "Come on, let's take a look inside."

Drawing the Luger pistol I had captured on D-Day, I led the way down the trench. A canvas door covered the entrance to the dugout. Pulling it gently away, I peered inside. The roof and walls had been reinforced with timber beams. An officer was looking through a pair of huge periscopic binoculars that disappeared into the roots of the tree above. Nearby, a second man sat in front of a gently humming radio, the aerial of which also disappeared through the roof, presumably into the branches of the tree. On a table was a field telephone, an artillery plotting board and a number of papers. It was all very ingenious.

"*Guten abend, Herren!* (Good evening, gentlemen!)," I said, pushing my way inside. "*Hände hoch – schnell!* (Hands up – quickly!)"

The pair of them spun round. The officer began reaching for his pistol, saw my Luger and Baker's Sten, thought better of it and raised his hands as he had been told. I could see from their badges that they belonged to the Waffen SS, who were Nazi troops fanatically loyal to Hitler. The ordinary German soldier fought by the rules (and we respected them for it), but these people did not. They would play dead in their foxholes until we had passed, then shoot us in the back, or pretend to surrender then open fire again, or shoot our stretcher bearers when they were attending to their wounded as well as our own. We showed them no mercy on these occasions and they did not seem to want it.

"Take half the patrol and escort the prisoners back to our lines," I said to Corporal Baker. "And send Haggerty in, will you? He can help me carry some of this stuff back."

"Yessir," replied Baker. "Just a thought, but if they turn funny and we have to shoot them, that could mean trouble for you back here."

"Yes, you're quite right, given their reputation," I said. "Tell you what, cut their braces and trouser buttons, then they'll have to keep their hands in their pockets. They'll not be much of a threat with their pants dangling round their ankles!"

Grinning, Baker did as I suggested. The officer, whose SS rank I took to be the equivalent of major, was about to make a vigorous protest but quietened down when Haggerty put the point of a trench knife under his chin. As the prisoners and their escort faded into the darkness, I took a look through the binoculars. Even in faint moonlight I could see every detail of our positions. For the past few days any movement on our side of the lines had immediately attracted accurate shellfire; now I knew why. The binoculars and their stand were too big to move, so I contented myself with smashing the lenses. While I did so, Haggerty opened the box that Bauer had delivered.

"Scoff, sir," he said. "It's not bad. Try some."

The box contained a flask of coffee, coarse grey bread, sausage and two boiled eggs. The coffee, which I believe was made from acorns, was dreadful, as was the bread, but the sausage and eggs weren't too bad. As I collected together the enemy's range tables, code books and list of radio frequencies, Haggerty did a good job of putting the radio out of action. Suddenly the field telephone gave a muted buzz. I wondered whether I should answer it and decided that it would seem strange if I didn't. I guessed that in such close proximity to our lines its users spoke in a whisper, which made it less likely that I would be identified. I picked up the receiver.

"*Ja?* (Yes?)"

"*Ist Bauer da, Herr Sturmbannführer?* (Is Bauer there, Major, sir?)"

"*Ja, ja, Bauer ist hier* (Yes, yes, Bauer is here)," I lied. No doubt they were wondering where he had got to.

"*Gut. Hauptsturmführer Klinger wird mit Ihnen in fünf minuten Sein.* (That's good. Captain Klinger will be with you in five minutes.)"

"*Danke* (Thanks)," I said, and rang off, not wishing to prolong a risky conversation.

"There'll be an SS captain arriving in five minutes," I told Haggerty. "My guess is that he's the Major's relief and if so he'll be bringing his radio operator with him. Tell the chaps outside to let them through, then close in behind them."

Five minutes later the canvas curtain was pulled aside.

"*Alles in ordnung?* (Everything in order?)," said a cheery voice.

"*Für mich ja - für Sie, nein!* (For me, yes – for you, no!)" I said in German as I spun round, thrusting my pistol into the startled officer's face.

Before the look of bewilderment had left their faces, the Captain and his radio operator were grabbed from behind. While their braces and trouser buttons were being cut, I gathered up the various books and papers I had assembled, stuffing them into a briefcase the Major had left behind.

"Come on, let's go," I said. "We're in danger of outstaying our welcome."

The return journey did not take as long as our outward march, partly because the moon was setting and partly because we had already cleared the trip wires off our path. Our standing patrol on the bank of the stream confirmed that Corporal Baker had come in and taken his prisoners to company headquarters. I did likewise, and from there they were marched off to be interrogated by the battalion's Intelligence Officer, who was also greatly interested in the documents I had brought in.

Duncan Flint was grinning from ear to ear, a sight I had never seen before.

"Can't do a darn thing right, can you, Andy?" he said. "I told you I wanted a prisoner and you walk in with five!"

"Thought you'd be glad of the company," I replied.

"Well done – it won't be forgotten, I promise you. Now go and get some sleep."

During the next few days the enemy's artillery fire was noticeably less intense, and certainly less accurate. A week after the patrol I was summoned again to company headquarters, where I found Colonel Armitage and the Brigade Commander.

"Ah, the young man himself," said the Brigadier as I entered. "You've done well, Andy. In fact you've been Mentioned in Despatches. I thought you deserved more but the divisional commander is a bit old-fashioned – believes that officers don't need medals to perform their duty."

I was handed the citation which said that a patrol led by Second Lieutenant Andrew Pope had eliminated an enemy artillery observation post, taken several prisoners and captured a number of important documents as a result of which the artillery fire-plan and signals network of the SS Panzergrenadier Division *Nibelungen* had been severely disrupted.

"That's just the way it worked out, sir," I said. "We were lucky, that's all."

"Results are what counts," replied the Brigadier. "Anyway, the Divisional Commander has agreed to bring forward your promotion, which isn't due for several months yet. Well done."

"Keep it up, Andy," said the Colonel, patting me on the back as he followed the Brigadier out.

"You're improperly dressed," said Duncan Flint, handing me a pair of pips. "Put these on – you're a full lieutenant now. Apart from which, I don't much care for second lieutenants."

"So I gathered," I replied. For a moment I almost liked him.

17 – 19 August 1944

By the beginning of August 1944 there had been definite signs that our efforts were beginning to pay off. We learned that Rommel had been evacuated to Germany after being seriously wounded, and that Hitler had narrowly survived an assassination attempt by some of his generals. The Americans had broken out of their beach-head and were swinging round the German left flank, which was being bent steadily backwards. Using new tactics, the British and Canadian armies began to push back the enemy's right flank to the north of Caen, so that by the middle of August both ends of the enemy line had been bent back so that the line itself resembled a sack. The Germans were now struggling desperately to hold open the neck of this so that they could escape eastwards.

We were enjoying a spell out of the line when the officers were called to a briefing by Colonel Armitage. He told us that the battalion had been ordered to seize a village called St Marc les Trois Ponts, situated directly on the enemy's escape route. The village lay on a hill enclosed in a loop of a river. Bridges crossed the river into the village on its east, south and west sides. During a night attack, we were to enter the village from the north, riding in Armoured Personnel Carriers (APCs). The attack would be spearheaded by tanks moving behind a heavy artillery barrage while the RAF suppressed opposition on the flanks with carpet bombing. Once a hole had been punched in the enemy front we would pass through it, enter the village and hold it against all comers until we were relieved. The result would be that a block would be placed across the enemy's escape route.

"Ha! It's a Death or Glory job, sir!" remarked Sergeant Warriner after I passed on the orders to the Platoon. "Difficult enough with a full battalion, but we're badly under strength."

That was true enough. The company now numbered about 80 men. My platoon, 25-strong, was the largest, but of those who had landed with me on D-Day only 15 remained, and some of them had returned to us after being wounded. I had also lost most of the original NCOs, either as casualties or because they had been sent to make up losses in other platoons. I had an uneasy feeling about this operation, but if someone higher up the chain of command had decided that we were expendable, there was nothing I could do about it.

*

We climbed aboard the APCs as dusk was falling on the evening of 18 August. For once, A Company was last in the battalion column. The attached artillery Forward Observation Officer (FOO), a Captain Paddy O'Connor, tagged on behind us in his Stuart light tank. Two squadrons of Shermans clattered past to deploy across the head of the column. We began to move forward, slowly but steadily. The artillery was already at work, pounding the enemy's front line. Right on time, flights of heavy bombers droned overhead to release tons of bombs on farms, woods and other possible strongpoints on either side of our route. Few could have survived in those rectangles of erupting earth flames and smoke as more and more aircraft released their bombs into the same target areas. Now I knew why the RAF called it carpet bombing.

The column came to a standstill. From ahead came the noise of tank guns. Distant flames indicated burning tanks, but whether they were our own or the enemy's I had no idea. From garbled talk on the APC's radio I gathered that the Shermans had run on to a newly laid minefield and were being engaged by the enemy's anti-tank guns and tanks. Time passed without any further movement forward. As the bombers turned for home it began to seem as though the operation would fail before it had really begun.

"ALL STATIONS ONE – FOLLOW ME!" Duncan Flint's

voice cracked like a whip in my earphones. "SHELLDRAKE CONFORM! OUT."

Shelldrake was the codename for the FOO. As the company's five APCs swung off the road to the right, I looked round and saw that his Stuart was following us. It seemed that the Major had studied his map and spotted a route to the objective across country, using farm tracks and minor roads, although this took us through one of the areas that the RAF had subjected to carpet bombing. I heard him call Colonel Armitage to advise him of this, but there was no response. We did not know it at the time, but in trying to work his way round the tank battle, the Colonel's APC had struck a mine and the shock of the explosion had thrown his radio off the frequency we were using. If we had known, we would probably have halted instead of proceeding deep into enemy territory on our own.

As soon as we reached the devastated area, the APCs began to buck, pitch and roll in the bomb craters. It took all the drivers' skill to get us through this smoking lunar landscape. Those of the enemy who had survived were too dazed to offer resistance. Some disappeared into the darkness, but most stood with their hands raised. Ignoring them, we pressed on, making better time along the farm tracks. The winding course of the river came into view, shining in the moonlight. At length we halted just short of the road leading into St Marc from the north and left the

APCs, which Duncan Flint ordered to return by the way we had come.

As we entered the village I could hear the sound of many wheels and horses' hooves on the cobbles. At the top of the main street a steady procession of horse-drawn enemy supply wagons was crossing the little square by the church. It was obvious that they had entered the village by the bridge to the west and would leave it by that leading east. Duncan Flint wasted no time. He instantly ordered the whole company to make a bayonet charge up the street. Confronted by a swarm of yelling figures emerging from the darkness, the transport drivers surrendered at once. I was instructed to continue the attack down the street leading to the western bridge, where we captured more wagons and their drivers. Across the river I could see a long stream of traffic was waiting to cross, including more horse-drawn wagons and a number of motor lorries. I opened fire on these. When the fuel tank of one of the lorries exploded, the light of the blazing vehicle revealed frantic men running in every direction for cover.

I attended a quick orders group at the church while Sergeant Warriner put the houses nearest the bridge into a defensible state by barricading the windows and doors. The FOO's Stuart was parked alongside the church vestry, which was now Company HQ. Duncan Flint said that he expected the rest of the battalion to join us soon. In the meantime, each platoon would guard one of the bridges and contribute five men to cover the way we had entered the village. The horses were to be turned loose and the wagons used to form barricades across the streets.

"What about the prisoners?" I asked.

"We haven't the manpower to guard 'em, so send them back where they came from. Chances are they'll say there are more of us here than there are. You can expect probing attacks, but because the river is on three sides of the village these can only be directed at the bridges."

"What about behind us?" asked Nigel.

"My guess is that the people to the north of us already have their hands full," the Major replied. "Nevertheless, I'm keeping an eye on the situation."

The probing attacks began an hour later. There were bursts of firing from Sergeant Brumby's One Platoon at the southern bridge, followed by more firing from Sergeant Mason's Two Platoon at the eastern bridge. I guessed that it would be our turn next. The burning lorry was no longer giving much light so I sent up flares from time to time. One of these showed a score of crouched figures running across the bridge. They were caught in the crossfire of our three Brens, the leaders being cut down at once. None of those who tried to escape across the bridge reached the other side. Quiet descended once more on the village. The thought struck me that our situation was similar to that of the position held by Duncan Flint's company at Tobruk, which had been protected by two wadis and a cliff. An hour before dawn I was summoned to another orders group. As I hurried up the street the frightened faces of the village's inhabitants peered at me from their cellar windows.

Duncan Flint was standing on the church steps when the rest of us arrived.

"There has been an unfortunate development, gentlemen," he began. "The battalion has been heavily counter-attacked and I do not know how long it will be before it will join us. Meanwhile, we are sitting right on one of Jerry's lines of retreat and, his probing attacks having failed, he will try and use some of his armour to dislodge us. I believe that you'll be hit first, Andy, and—"

His words were drowned by the scream of an incoming salvo of shells. There was an explosion in the church doorway and I remember being hurled through the air – then blackness. I do not think that I was unconscious for more than a few seconds. I was aware of running feet and the sound of Sergeant Brumby's voice.

"Take 'em down to the crypt under the church, lads. Joe, have look at Mr Pope."

I opened my eyes to see Sergeant Mason looking down at me.

"You hit, sir?" he asked.

All my limbs seemed to be in working order but I had

a splitting headache. Soldiers were carrying bloodstained figures down the steps into the crypt. More figures were sprawled on the cobbles. There seemed to be blood everywhere. I sat up slowly, shaking my head.

"What's happening?"

"The Major's been badly hit, sir," answered Sergeant Mason. "So has the Artillery Officer. I'm afraid Captain Wood is dead, so is Sergeant Major Darracott and Barnes, the Company Signaller."

I stood up unsteadily. Obviously, those who had been standing on the other side of the orders group had absorbed the worst of the shell's effects.

"You're in command, now, sir," said Sergeant Brumby in a matter-of-fact voice.

The shock of our loss was bad enough, but suddenly I felt crushed by the immense weight of the additional responsibility thrust upon me. I was commanding an under-strength company that was doing a battalion's job behind enemy lines, and whatever happened had become my responsibility. The two sergeants were looking at me expectantly.

"Send someone to fetch Sergeant Warriner," I heard my voice say. My ingrained training and discipline were asserting themselves automatically. "Tell him to bring Corporal Baker and Helsby-Frodsham with him – at the double!"

Sporadic shelling continued to strike the village, so I moved the orders group to the narrow space between the vestry and the parked Stuart. Shortly after, the others arrived.

"Sergeant Warriner, you'll take over as company sergeant major," I said. "Corporal Baker, you are now commanding Three Platoon. Helsby-Frodsham, you are responsible for the company signals net."

They nodded, obviously aware of what had happened.

"Now, the Major's opinion was that we would be attacked by armour shortly," I continued. "I agree with that, and also that Three Platoon is most likely to be hit first. This is what we are going to do. There's a china shop round the corner. It contains a supply of round, earthenware casserole dishes. Lay them upside down in a pattern across the square. With any luck Jerry will think they are anti-tank mines, especially if we get someone to paint a sign saying ACHTUNG – MINEN! Sergeant Warriner, would you attend to that?"

"Sir!" Sergeant Warriner did not bat an eyelid at the changed circumstances.

"What about us, sir?" asked Sergeant Brumby.

"Collect as many bottles and jars as you can and make Molotov cocktails with them. Use the petrol in the Stuart, but leave enough for the engine to charge the tank's radio batteries or we're sunk. Supplement it with paraffin, lamp oil, any liquid that will burn.

"When the attack develops, keep your men out of sight. Jerry may think we've pulled out – if so, well and good. With any luck, his leading vehicle will halt at our 'minefield'. At that point, your PIAT will knock it out, Sergeant Mason. Simultaneously, Corporal Baker, your PIAT will knock out the last vehicle in the column. That will leave the rest of them trapped between the two. At that point, and not before, we tackle them with our Molotov cocktails, as well as any infantry who happen to be escorting them. Any questions?"

They shook their heads.

"All right, we'd all better get on with it. I calculate that we've only 30 minutes of darkness left."

No sooner had they left than Helsby-Frodsham reported that the company's radio linking us to the battalion was smashed beyond repair. We therefore decided that he would operate the company's internal radio net while we tried to establish a new link using the artillery set in the Stuart.

I clambered aboard the tank, where the FOO's operator, Bombardier Seward, a very capable and experienced NCO, was sitting beside his set. He told me that, subject to my orders, he could probably get us fire support when we needed it. He showed me a map board already marked by the FOO in which the three bridges had been given codewords, as were various crossroads, farms and woods in enemy territory.

"All I have to do is send the codeword and the guns will do the rest, sir," he said. "It may not be as accurate as it would be if Captain O'Connor was controlling the shoot, but it will be near enough."

He also said that a message could be relayed on the artillery's radio frequency to brigade headquarters and then to our battalion, although it would take time. I handed him a scribbled note to send:

ONE FOR NINE. SUNRAY DOWN ALSO SUNRAY MINOR AND SHELLDRAKE. AM PROCEEDING WITH MISSION BUT EXPECT MAJOR ATTACK SHORTLY. OUT.

"One" was the A Company callsign and "nine" was the battalion control set, while the words "Sunray" and "Sunray Minor" indicated the company commander and his second-in-command.

I climbed the church tower just as day was breaking. Looking south, I could see a long line of enemy traffic that had by-passed the village moving across country. It included horse-drawn transport and guns as well as motor vehicles of every type. A massive jam was building up where it attempted to join another traffic stream heading east. Further south, I could see shells bursting and guessed that they were probably fired by the Americans as they strove to close the enemy's escape route from their side. A roar of powerful aero engines signified the arrival of a squadron of rocket-firing Typhoons that pounced on the stalled lines of vehicles. Explosions erupted along the columns and fires sprang up. Through my binoculars I watched tiny figures running across the fields. It seemed that we were doing our job and I was determined to see it through.

"Sir, Sergeant Brumby says there's a Jerry officer with a flag of truce at the south bridge," shouted Helsby-Frodsham up the belfry ladder. "Wants a word with whoever is in charge."

I deliberately took my time walking down to the bridge, in the middle of which stood an impatient-looking German colonel and a soldier with a white flag on a stick. We exchanged salutes.

"What do you want?" I asked.

"I wish to speak with your commanding officer," he replied in clipped, precise English. "This is not a matter for a mere lieutenant."

"Well, he's having his breakfast and doesn't want to talk to you," I lied. "By the way, I think my German is better than your English, so let's converse in that."

It wasn't, of course, but saying so gave me a slight advantage and clearly annoyed the Colonel.

"I am here to offer honourable surrender terms," he said.

His face wore a haggard, desperate expression that I decided to exploit.

"Splendid, Colonel," I replied. "If you would kindly get your men to throw their weapons in the river and form up in that field we shall deal with them in due course."

His face went purple with rage.

"You young fool, don't you understand? I am here to demand *your* surrender!" he bellowed.

"Out of the question," I said, feigning astonishment. "And we both know that you're not really in a position to demand anything, are you?"

"Very well, you have had your chance, *Herr Leutnant*," he snarled. "When your men are slaughtered the responsibility will be yours!"

"Good morning to you," I replied, turning on my heel.

Sergeant Warriner was waiting for me when I returned to the church. I gave him the details of my conversation with the German, at which he gave his short laugh.

"You can't blame him for trying, sir!" he remarked. "By the way, I've found a French doctor who is willing to look after the wounded, sir," he said. "Two of the women have nursing experience and they're willing to help, too."

"Do they know that Jerry will probably shoot them if things go badly for us?"

"They're willing to take a chance, and we'll need 'em." He stood looking thoughtful for a while before he continued.

131

"Couple of things bothering me, sir. We've only enough ammunition for one good engagement, and we're holding too much ground for a company."

"Well, there are plenty of captured weapons lying about, so we'll use those first. I agree about our perimeter, though. My plan is to deny the enemy the bridges for as long as possible, then fall back on the square. That way we'll still be able to stop them using the route through the village."

"Very good, sir." The Sergeant's tone was non-committal. "I'll have the men collect the abandoned Jerry arms and ammo. Rations aren't a problem – there's a baker's round the corner, and a butcher's too, so I've requisitioned some of their stock and distributed it."

Bombardier Seward appeared in the turret of the Stuart.

"Your message has been acknowledged, sir," he called. "I'll let you know as soon as the reply comes through."

I climbed up beside him, consulted my map and scribbled a six-figure grid reference on a message pad.

"This is our position, including the church, the churchyard and the square," I said, handing it to him. "Get your chaps to add it to their list of targets. The codeword will be VENICE. Use the Slidex code when you send, of course."

I had learned the Slidex code at OCTU and knew that if enemy operators were listening it would be almost impossible for them to crack it on the basis of one transmission.

"Are things that bad, sir?" Seward replied, eyeing the pad dubiously. Normally, one only called down artillery fire on one's own position in extreme circumstances.

"No, but we may as well be prepared."

Helsby-Frodsham poked his head out of the vestry door.

"The Major's asking for you, sir."

In the crypt the French doctor and his volunteer nurses were doing what they could for our wounded. The doctor told me that Duncan Flint was drifting in and out of consciousness at the moment and was very seriously injured. His back, left arm and left leg were swathed in bandages through which blood was soaking.

"Ah, Andy, there . . . you are," he said. It was obvious that speech was difficult and painful for him. "Now listen carefully . . . this is what you've to do. . ."

"I'm sorry, Major, but I'm in command now. You've been badly hurt and must get all the rest you can."

He glared at me balefully.

"In command . . . are you? What . . . are your plans . . . then?"

"I'm going to hold the village as long as I can. If we look like being overrun I'm going to pull everyone back here into the crypt, then call down an artillery strike on top of us. When that's lifted we'll break out and rejoin the battalion."

"Good ... I would have ... done ... the same. Not altogether ... wasted my time with ... you, it seems. I've seen ... my company ... march into captivity once. Don't want ... to see it again. Just don't ... mess up, laddie."

It was hardly a vote of confidence, but he was drifting into unconsciousness and I bit back a sharp reply. I climbed the tower again. To the south the American shell bursts seemed much closer and our aircraft were harrying the enemy columns without mercy. I was witnessing the death of the German Army in Normandy. From the north came the sounds of intense fighting as the rest of our battalion tried to break through to us. I began to wonder whether the German Colonel's threats had simply been bluster, although from time to time salvos of shells continued to land in the village, wrecking houses and setting one ablaze. Sergeant Warriner joined me. By shouting instructions to Seward, we were able to bring down our own shells on areas in which the enemy might be forming up for an attack.

"Slidex message, sir," said Helsby-Frodsham from the top of the belfry ladder. He handed me the message pad. "The Bombardier's decoded it for you."

The message read: CRUMPETS FOR TEA USUAL TIME EARLIER IF POSSIBLE.

"What's it mean, sir?" asked Sergeant Warriner.

"I think it means that the battalion will have broken through to us by 16:15. That's the time we used to have tea in the Mess. It's coming up to noon now, so we've about four hours to wait, unless Jerry decides to attack us after all."

"He has, sir! Take a look!" Warriner exclaimed, pointing.

A large force of enemy infantry were moving stealthily along the north bank of the river, using trees and hedges for cover. They obviously intended attacking the open end of the village, using the same route we had entered it by. It was here that our defences were weakest.

"Tell Sergeant Mason to send one of his sections across to the north end of the village!" I shouted down to Helsby-Frodsham, then turned to Sergeant Warriner. "Go and take charge there yourself. There's only a narrow gap between the two bends in the river and I don't think Jerry will be able to deploy his full strength for an attack there. I'll reinforce you if necessary."

I had the sickening feeling that somehow I had made a terrible mistake. The sounds of heavy fighting still came from the north, so where had this attack come from? I glanced quickly at the map and saw that a weir was marked two miles downstream. Obviously the enemy had crossed there on foot. I cursed myself for not noticing it earlier. Yet, they could not have known that the north end of the village was our weakest point, and would have been aware that they could only attack on a limited frontage. If this was a diversion where would the main attack be delivered?

Seconds later I knew the answer. Four low-slung assault guns were moving along the road towards the west bridge. Behind each trotted a squad of infantry, with yet more infantry beyond them. I rejected at once any idea that our Stuart should engage them, for its little 37mm gun was no match for the assault guns' long 75mm cannon, apart from which its radio was our only link with the outside world. I shouted for Seward to bring down shellfire on the west bridge, and for Helsby-Frodsham to tell Corporal Baker to keep his men hidden in accordance with our plan. Already I could hear the crackle of rifle fire and the stutter of Brens as Sergeant Warriner's men began beating off the diversionary assault.

The assault guns passed through the rain of shells apparently unscathed. The leading vehicle fired in turn at each of the overturned supply wagons we were using as barricades, then pushed its way through the splintered wreckage. As it reached the square its driver, spotting our "minefield", halted, uncertain what to do. Immediately, a PIAT bomb slammed into the side of the vehicle, its blast killing those within. A second bomb hit the rearmost vehicle, which shuddered to a standstill with smoke pouring from its engine compartment. Then all hell seemed to break loose. Three Platoon appeared at the windows of houses on both sides of the street, hurling Molotov cocktails and blazing away with their weapons. The assault guns' infantry escort were cut down, as were the crews attempting to escape from their burning vehicles.

The west to east route through the village was now successfully blocked, but as our artillery concentration on the west bridge lifted, more and more of the German infantry swarmed across, fanning out to the right and left so that they outflanked the positions held by Sergeant Brumby and Sergeant Warriner. I descended the tower just as Corporal Baker signalled that he had lost two houses near the bridge. I told Helsby-Frodsham to call the platoon commanders and tell them that they should fall back slowly on the church, but make the enemy pay for every yard of ground. He was to add that on hearing three long blasts on my whistle they were to break contact and run for the church.

"MAKE SURE EVERYONE KNOWS WHAT YOU'RE DOING," said a sudden voice in my head. I put it down to fatigue, but it was just the sort of annoying remark Duncan Flint would make when I had already decided to do something.

It had now become a soldier's battle. There was nothing more I could do at this stage, so I snatched up a machine pistol and several magazines from a dead German lying beside an assault gun, and visited each platoon in turn. I cannot recall the details, but the fighting was bitter. It raged in the streets, through houses, from barricade to barricade and across gardens. The Germans were fighting to break out of a trap, but we were fighting for our survival and that gave us an edge.

Heavily outnumbered, we were forced back slowly, which was good in one way as we had less ground to hold. On the other hand, we were losing men steadily and had fewer to hold it with. During each lull I managed to gather half a dozen men together as a reserve and used it to recapture a house or barricade with a counter-attack. I lost track of time but at length it became apparent that we would be overrun. Sergeant Warriner's group had already fallen back to the north wall of the churchyard. Corporal Baker and Three Platoon were already pulling back to the west wall. One and Two Platoons were retreating doggedly but were being pressed hard. The danger was that they would be swamped by the next enemy assault, and that would leave us with too few men to hold the churchyard. Worse, this was the moment I should have called down our own artillery, but I could not leave them exposed to it. I already had my whistle in my mouth when I heard the voice again: "NOW! BRING 'EM IN BEFORE IT'S TOO LATE! YOU HAVEN'T A SECOND TO SPARE!"

I blew three long blasts. The men came streaming in,

pursued by the enemy's fire. I saw Sergeant Brumby run to the leading assault gun, which had been knocked out in the centre of the square. He clambered on to the superstructure, where a Spandau machine-gun was mounted beside the commander's hatch. He immediately opened fire on the Germans massing in the streets leading to the south and west bridges, scything through them and forcing them to dive for cover.

"Back to the church!" I yelled at the two platoons. "Barricade the doors when everyone is inside and go down to the crypt!"

As they ran past me I turned to Sergeant Brumby. "Come on – you've done enough!" I shouted. "Get inside – I'm calling down an artillery strike!"

"I'll just see the lads safely inside, sir!" he replied as he continued to blaze away. "Don't worry about me!"

Bullets were already ricocheting off the gun shield and the assault gun's armour as I ran to the Stuart.

"Call for VENICE now!" I yelled at Bombardier Seward. "Then get out of there and into the church!"

As we squeezed through the last gap in the church's big double doors I glanced across the square. Sergeant Brumby was lying slumped across the machine-gun, his blood running down the assault gun's side. The doors slammed shut and were barricaded with anything we could lay our hands on. In the crypt, we did likewise with the door connecting it to the church. The doctor and his nurses were hard at work in the hot, over-crowded space. A small door in the wall of the crypt gave access to a flight of steps leading up to the churchyard. I ordered the fit men to assemble by it and told them that as soon as our bombardment had lifted we would use these to assemble behind the north wall of the churchyard.

"We'll go over it together," I said. "I'm counting on Jerry being too dazed to do anything, but don't stop for anyone or anything. The rest of the battalion is heading this way and we should be able to break through to them."

From above came the sound of the enemy battering on the church door, together with the tinkle of breaking glass and explosions as they flung grenades into the building. I went over to Duncan Flint and to my horror saw that his face was now covered by a blanket. Shaking his head sadly, the French doctor told me that he had died only minutes after my last visit. The men had liked him, and I decided to keep this news to myself for the moment. Although I had never really liked him, I felt a terrible sense of loss, for A Company was his creation and now he had gone.

I glanced at my watch. It said four o'clock. I felt bitterly disappointed that we had not been able to hold out for another fifteen minutes, because the rest of the battalion would have arrived by then. Then came the scream of the first salvo of shells. What followed seemed to go on for ever.

The earth round us seemed to heave as salvo followed salvo. From above came the sound of crashing masonry and the shattering of glass as the huge windows were blown in. In the crypt, dust was shaken from every crevice and hung in the air like a fog. I expected the church floor to collapse on to us any minute, but the stout stone Norman columns continued to support it. Then there was silence.

"Come on!" I yelled, wrenching the door open and charging up the steps. I emerged into a scene from hell. Part of the church wall had collapsed, bringing much of the roof down as well. German bodies, many of them dismembered, lay everywhere. Shattered gravestones and monuments littered the ground. Skeletal remains could be seen in some of the craters. The occupant of an uprooted coffin grinned bonily at me as I ran past. I reached the north wall and heard the thud of boots as the others joined me. I peered over. The enemy, severely shaken, had pulled back into the surrounding gardens to regroup and reorganize. To my surprise, shells began to burst among them.

"Look, sir!" shouted Sergeant Warriner, pointing.

A squadron of Sherman tanks, deployed in line, was approaching the village, firing as they advanced. Some way behind was the battalion's leading company, riding in APCs. As the enemy turned to face this new attack, two strange vehicles detached themselves from the tank squadron and closed in on the end of the street. Through my binoculars

I was able to identify them as Churchills, although they were towing armoured trailers. Suddenly a great tongue of flame belched out of one. It lasted for several seconds and stretched half the length of the street, setting everything in its path ablaze. I had heard of the terrible Crocodile flamethrowers, but never seen them before. Smashing their way through the barricades, they advanced slowly and with infinite menace. I could see the enemy's fire ricocheting uselessly off their armour. Another belch of flame, this time reaching the edge of the square and sticking to anything it touched. Many of the enemy fled, but most flung down their arms and surrendered.

Beside me, our men were cheering and waving their helmets. The Crocodiles reached the square, shunted the derelict assault gun aside and turned south to cross the bridge into what had been enemy territory. The Shermans followed in their wake. Then came our own B Company, the commander of which, Major James Masterson, stopped briefly beside me.

"Ye gods, young Andy, what's been going on here?" he asked, looking around the scene of carnage and desolation. "Anything I can do to help out?"

"I'd be glad if you'd drop off a few of your blokes, sir," I replied. "We've a lot of wounded and there's prisoners to guard."

"Will do," he said. "Sorry I can't stop – got an appointment with our American cousins. Seems they've closed the enemy's last escape route and it's just about all over."

The rest of the battalion passed through. The wounded, the enemy's as well as our own, were taken out to a fleet of ambulances that had arrived. The prisoners were marshalled and I made arrangements for our own men to have a brew of tea and a hot meal. The church tower was still more or less intact, so when these administrative tasks had been attended to Sergeant Warriner and I climbed to the top. We watched in silence as, to the south, British and American red and green recognition flares went up and white flags began fluttering along the stalled enemy columns. Typhoons flew overhead, ready to pounce on any remaining signs of resistance.

"Damn fine show, Andy, damn fine!" said a voice. We turned to see Colonel Armitage clambering out of the hatch. "You can tell A Company how proud I am of them – and so is the Brigadier and the General!"

"Thank you, Colonel, they'll appreciate that," I replied. "I'm afraid there are less than fifty of us left on our feet."

"That's hard to bear, I know," he said, looking out at the surrendering German Army. "Nevertheless, several thousand of those people could have made their escape through this village during the time you've been here, then been used to fight against us again. You must balance your loss against that."

He paused for a minute, looking down at the ambulances moving off.

"I'm sorry about Duncan, Nigel and the others," he continued, turning to look me straight in the eye. "Duncan was a difficult man to command and I'm sure he was a difficult man to serve under, but he produced results and that's what counts. He thought that you showed great promise, by the way, although he'd never have told you so."

I was surprised but did not think it appropriate to comment, so I simply nodded.

"Oh, one other thing, Andy," said the Colonel as he began to descend the ladder. "If you care to give me a list of names for suitable awards I'll give it my full backing."

"Too bad about the Major, sir," commented Sergeant Warriner after a few moments' reflection. "I suppose that last effort was too much for him. Should have stayed in the crypt with the rest of the wounded."

"What do you mean?" I asked, taken aback.

"As we ran in I saw him standing behind you in the square."

I felt the hairs rise on the back of my neck.

"Major Flint had been dead for nearly four hours by then. The doctor will confirm that. Did you see him after we'd pulled back into the church?"

"No, sir," replied the Sergeant, a look of bewilderment crossing his face. "But I did see him standing behind you in the square just as clearly as I'm seeing you now. I'll take my oath on it!"

Warriner was an honest man, not given to too much imagination, and I knew that he was telling the truth.

"Wouldn't let go, would he?" I said, at length.

"Looks that way, sir," he replied, in his matter-of-fact way. "Wanted to be sure the company was in good hands, that's all. When he was satisfied, he left us. That's the only explanation I can offer. Now I don't know where soldiers go when they die, sir, but wherever it is he'll be grateful to you."

Shortly after, another battalion from the brigade arrived to take over the village from us. I marched what was left of A Company to a nearby field where we spent the night. I found it difficult to sleep until I realized why. For the first time since D-Day the sound of the guns was absent. The silence was uncanny.

Epilogue

To my sorrow, A Company was never re-formed. Following the great Allied victory in Normandy, our armoured divisions swept north to liberate Belgium while the Americans embarked on a whirlwind advance to the German frontier. During this period we were told that our entire division was to be disbanded and used to reinforce other divisions. The problem was that the United Kingdom's manpower resources had become stretched to their limits.

My recommendations for awards won during the battle for St Marc were accepted in full. Sergeant Brumby, but for whose self-sacrifice we might have been overrun, received the posthumous award of the Victoria Cross. Sergeant Warriner, who had commanded the most difficult sector of the defences as well as acting as company sergeant major throughout, added a Distinguished Conduct Medal (DCM) to his Military Medal (MM). As he had been involved in active service throughout the Desert War and from D-Day onwards I felt that he had done enough and this was also accepted. He was confirmed in the rank of sergeant major and posted to a training regiment in England. I am not sure whether he was grateful or not. Sergeant Mason, later killed in Holland, received the MM, as did Corporal Baker, who rose to the rank of sergeant. He has recently been demobilized and returned to his family. A recommendation was passed to the Royal Artillery that Bombardier Seward, who had carried out his dead officer's task and ensured that we received artillery support when we needed it most, should receive the DCM, and I am pleased to say that this was approved. Several more men were Mentioned in Despatches.

Of the old Three Platoon hands, Grover has reached the rank of corporal and decided to remain in the Regular Army, where, at last, he seems to have found his niche in life. He is said to be a strict disciplinarian, but then he knows his own tricks best. Haggerty was promoted to lance corporal twice and lost his stripes on both occasions because of his illegal business activities. I am told that, but for his MM, he would have spent time in detention barracks. He has now returned to Liverpool, apparently a great deal richer than when he left it. Helsby-Frodsham received a serious leg wound during the closing stages of the action, rendering him unfit for further service in the infantry. Rather than have him idle his time away in some depot, I produced several brilliant water-colour sketches he had made of the fighting in Normandy and suggested that he was appointed an official war artist. The appointment was sanctioned and he recently came to see me with the news that he had been commissioned by the Regiment to paint the final stages of the battle for St Marc. I took Allen with me when I started my present job, fearing that no one else would put up with him. He has now returned to the Savoy Hotel and is probably driving its guests to distraction with his endless chatter.

As for myself, I was sent on a course to learn my duties as an Intelligence Officer, then joined my new brigade, of which the newly promoted Colonel Armitage is second-in-command. After a while, I was sent on a short leave to England. My parents accompanied me to Buckingham Palace, where the King presented me with the Military Cross. A shy, quietly spoken man with a slight stammer, he had obviously been briefed about the action at St Marc and asked me several well-informed questions about it. One could not help but like him.

For the rest of the War, most of my duties involved the interrogation of prisoners. When the fighting ended, I found myself interrogating Nazi Party officials, members of the Gestapo, and SS concentration camp guards. They were all guilty of horrific and inhuman acts. I do not know which of them I detested most – those who claimed that they were only obeying orders, or those who showed no shame at what they had done and went smirking to the gallows. They were evil personified and it had been worth fighting a war to rid the world of such men.

Historical note

The Allied invasion of Normandy, Operation Overlord, was the largest amphibious operation in history. It involved no less than 1,213 warships, 4,126 landing ships and landing craft, 736 support vessels and 864 merchant vessels, plus two pre-fabricated Mulberry harbours, which Andy mentions in his story. Air cover was provided by the combined might of the British and American tactical air forces, supplemented by the heavy bombers of the US Strategic Air Force. Prior to launching the invasion, elaborate deception measures successfully convinced the Germans that the Allied landings would take place in the Pas de Calais, which offered the shortest sea route between the United Kingdom and France. As a result, most of their armoured divisions were held back in this area. As the Allied troops moved to their embarkation ports, southern England was sealed off from the rest of the country for security reasons. Simultaneously, French Resistance groups attacked road and rail communications in northern France to hinder the movement of enemy reinforcements into the battle area.

After postponement due to bad weather, the date of the invasion, codenamed D-Day, was set for 6 June. Shortly after midnight, one British and two American airborne divisions were dropped to secure the flanks of the invasion area. The seaborne assault, under the overall command of General Sir Bernard Montgomery, commenced at 06:30, when the tide would leave the German beach obstacles exposed. On the right, Lieutenant General Omar Bradley's US First Army landed on two beaches designated Utah and Omaha; on the left, Lieutenant General Sir Miles Dempsey's British Second Army, including a large Canadian element, landed on beaches designated Gold, Juno and Sword. As Andy narrates, on the British and Canadian sectors the specialized armoured vehicles developed by the 79th Armoured Division proved invaluable in overcoming the enemy's beach defences and casualties were far lighter than had been expected. The Americans, however, lacking such vehicles, sustained over 3,000 killed and wounded on Omaha Beach alone. Nevertheless, by midnight, 57,000 American and 75,000 British and Canadian troops, plus their equipment, had been put ashore and the process of linking the beach-heads had begun. Allied losses amounted to 2,500 killed and 8,500 wounded; the full extent of German losses remains unknown.

The Allied strategy during the Normandy campaign was for the British and Canadians to maintain constant pressure on the enemy, thereby preventing the transfer of German reserves to the American sector, where the great breakout from the beach-head was planned. This meant that much of the fighting took place in close *bocage* country, where the Allies could not make full use of their armour. Consequently, losses among the infantry were high, sometimes approaching the level sustained during the Battle of the Somme in World War I. For their part, the Germans, who also lacked air cover, were handicapped by Hitler's "no withdrawal" orders and forced to endure the terrible effects of naval gunfire.

On 1 August the Americans broke out of the beach-head and began swinging round the enemy's left flank. Simultaneously, the British and Canadians began forcing back the enemy right flank, so that by the middle of the month the German armies in Normandy were trapped inside a shrinking pocket south of Falaise. The exit from the pocket was finally closed on 19 August. Some 10,000 Germans had died within it and 50,000 were captured. Also captured or destroyed were hundreds of tanks, self-propelled guns, armoured cars, artillery weapons and motor vehicles.

The episode involving Andy's batman, Private Allen, and the Tiger tank is based on a real incident that took place during the bitter battle for Hill 112. The operation to close an enemy escape route from the pocket is based on the actions fought at, respectively, St Lambert-sur-Dives and Mont Ormel, during the last stages of the campaign.

Early in his story Andy mentions that one of his ancestors, Michael Pope, served as a drummer boy during the Crimean War. Michael's adventures can be found in another *My Story* book, *Crimea*.

Timeline

19 August 1942 British and Canadian raid on Dieppe obtains much useful information regarding the nature of the German coastal defences.

6 June 1944 D-Day. US First and British Second Armies secure five beach-heads on the coast of Normandy.

7–12 June Beach-heads joined to form continuous 50-mile front.

19–22 June The Great Storm. American Mulberry harbour seriously damaged.

26 June–1 July Operation Epsom, the British Second Army's offensive across the Odon and Orne rivers south-west of Caen.

29 June Americans take Cherbourg.

9 July British take Caen.

18–21 July Operation Goodwood, the British Second Army's offensive south-east of Caen.

20 July Realizing that he was leading Germany to a terrible defeat, a group of senior German generals attempt to assassinate Hitler with a bomb planted in a briefcase.

They fail to kill him. He takes a ferocious revenge on them.

25 July Operation Cobra, the American break-out west of St Lô begins.

30 July Beginning of Operation Bluecoat, the British Second Army's offensive towards Mont Pincon and the Vire river, pinning down German troops ordered to oppose the American breakout.

6–7 August Americans beat off weak German counter-attack at Mortain. US Third Army turns German left flank. British capture Mont Pincon.

8–11 August Operation Totalize. First Canadian Army's offensive towards Falaise, Phase I.

14–16 August Operation Tractable, the First Canadian Army's offensive towards Falaise, Phase II, pushes in the German right flank. The German armies in Normandy are now trapped within a shrinking pocket south of Falaise.

17–19 August Trapped German armies struggle to escape eastwards but surrender when the last exit from the pocket is closed.

17–26 September Allied airborne operations in Holland secure bridges at Eindhoven and Nijmegen but end in gallant failure at Arnhem.

16 December 1944–16 January 1945 A major German counter-offensive in the Ardennes is defeated.

8 February–10 March The Allies secure the left bank of the River Rhine in Germany. The Americans capture the bridge at Remagen intact on 7 March.

22 March The Americans cross the Rhine in force at Oppenheim.

23 March The British cross the Rhine at Wesel.

30 April Hitler commits suicide in his bunker in Berlin.

2 May Berlin falls to the Russians who have arrived from the east. Advancing British and Russian armies make contact.

5–8 May Unconditional surrender of German armies in western Europe.

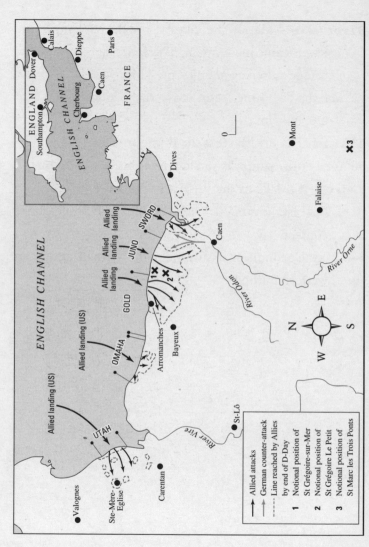

A map of the D-Day landings, 6 June 1944.

Allied troops going ashore in Normandy on 6th June, 1944. DD (Duplex Drive) Sherman tanks are already on the beach along with other armoured vehicles.

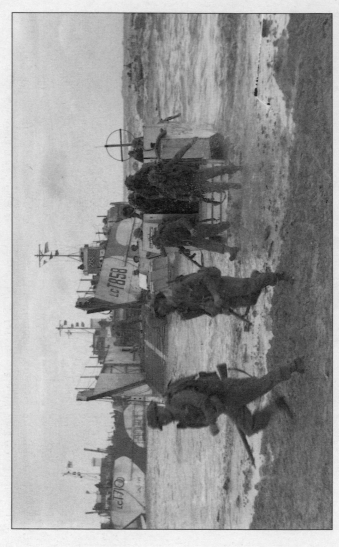

LCAs (Landing Craft Assault) transport Allied infantry from the LST (Landing Ship Tank) to the beach.

Allied troops landing. As the tide rises some have a longer wade ashore than others.

German prisoners beside a knocked-out Sherman Crab tank. The tide is rising but they are still stancing where they have been told to.

Allied infantry of the follow-up wave prepare to leave the beach on D-Day.

Amphibious lorries bringing supplies ashore. The barrage balloons, which can be seen in the distance, provided a defence against attacks by low-flying aircraft.

A 'Kangaroo' Armoured Personnel Carrier (APC) with infantry aboard. Like the real kangaroo, which carries its young in its pouch, this vehicle carried its passengers in a central compartment.

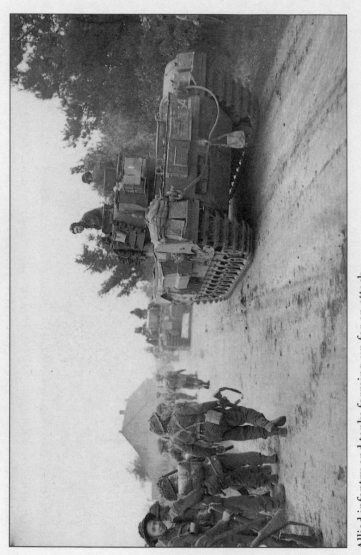

Allied infantry and tanks forming-up for an attack.

An AVRE (Armoured Vehicle Royal Engineers) carrying a fascine. Fascines would be used to fill anti-tank ditches so that vehiles could cross them.

Infantry and tank action in the *bocage*, a large area of countryside in Normandy.

Picture acknowledgements

All photographs reproduced by the kind permission of the Trustees of the Imperial War Museum, London.

P158 Map of the D-Day Landings, András Bereznay

Every effort has been made to trace the copyright holders and we apologize in advance for any unintentional omissions. We would be pleased to insert the appropriate acknowledgements in any subsequent edition of this book

Experience history first-hand with My Story – a series of
vividly imagined accounts of life in the past.

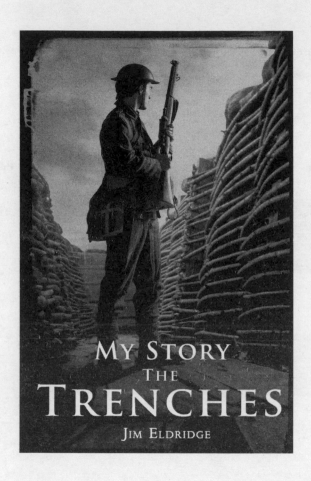

MY STORY
THE
TRENCHES

JIM ELDRIDGE

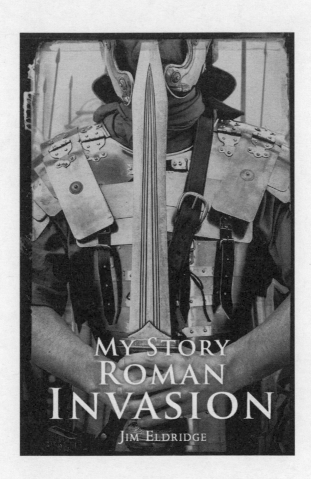

MY STORY
ROMAN
INVASION

JIM ELDRIDGE

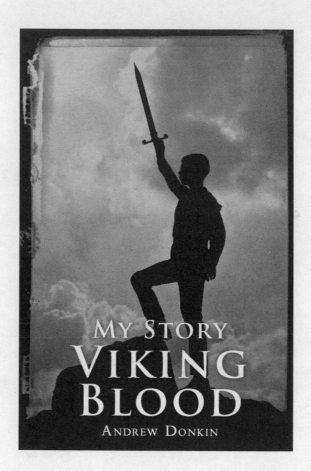

My Story

VIKING
BLOOD

Andrew Donkin

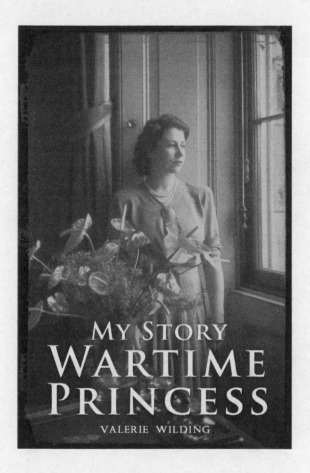

My Story
Wartime
Princess

VALERIE WILDING

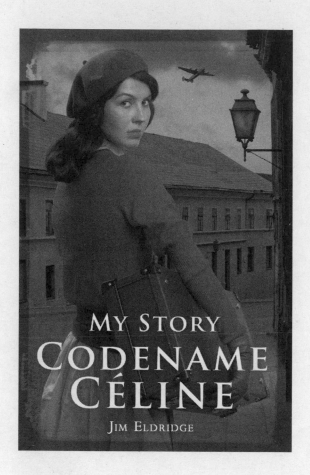

MY STORY
CODENAME
CÉLINE

JIM ELDRIDGE